Penguin Books

CW00351186

# The Golden Oriole

H. E. Bates was born in 1905 at Rushden in Northamptonshire and was educated at Kettering Grammar School. He worked as a journalist and clerk on a local newspaper before publishing his first book, *The Two Sisters*, when he was twenty. In the next fifteen years he acquired a distinguished reputation for his stories about English country life. During the Second World War, he was a Squadron Leader in the R.A.F. and some of his stories of service life, *The Greatest People in the World* (1942), *How Sleep the Brave* (1943) and *The Face of England* (1953), were written under the pseudonym of 'Flying Officer X'. His subsequent novels of Burma, *The Purple Plain* and *The Jacaranda Tree*, and of India, *The Scarlet Sword*, stemmed directly or indirectly from his war experience in the Eastern theatre of war.

In 1958 his writing took a new direction with the appearance of *The Darling Buds of May*, the first of the popular Larkin family novels, which was followed by *A Breath of French Air*, *When the Green Woods Laugh*, *Oh! To Be in England* and *A Little of What You Fancy*. The Larkin sequence is published in Penguin in one volume entitled *Perfick, Perfick!* His autobiography appeared in three volumes, *The Vanished World* (1969), *The Blossoming World* (1971) and *The World in Ripeness* (1972). His last works included the novel *The Triple Echo* (1971) and a collection of short stories, *The Song of the Wren* (1972). Perhaps one of his most famous works of fiction is the best-selling novel *Fair Stood the Wind for France* (1944). H. E. Bates also wrote miscellaneous works on gardening, essays on country life, several plays including *The Day of Glory* (1945); *The Modern Short Story* (1941) and a story for children, *The White Admiral* (1968). His works have been translated into sixteen languages and a posthumous collection of his stories, *The Yellow Meads of Asphodel*, appeared in 1976.

H. E. Bates was awarded the C.B.E. in 1973 and died in January 1974. He was married in 1931 and had four children.

# The Golden Oriole

H. E. Bates

Penguin Books
in association with Michael Joseph

Penguin Books Ltd, Harmondsworth, Middlesex, England
Viking Penguin Inc., 40 West 23rd Street, New York, New York 10010, U.S.A.
Penguin Books Australia Ltd, Ringwood, Victoria, Australia
Penguin Books Canada Limited, 2801 John Street, Markham, Ontario, Canada L3R 1B4
Penguin Books (N.Z.) Ltd, 182–190 Wairau Road, Auckland 10, New Zealand

First published by Michael Joseph 1962
Published in Penguin Books 1965
Reissued 1986

Copyright © Evensford Productions Ltd, 1962
All rights reserved

Printed and bound in Great Britain by
Cox & Wyman Ltd, Reading
Set in Monotype Bembo

# Contents

# The Ring of Truth

George Pickard, with a sickening start, woke for the fifth time in a month from a strange dream of his father, who had died suddenly six weeks before.

As always in the dream, his father was catching a train. It was midwinter and bitterly cold and the train, as always, was the night express to the North: sleeper coaches with drawn blinds, white steam from two big engines curdling into a black freezing sky, a strong air of suspense under the hooded yellow lights of an almost deserted platform No. 3.

His father had been a thin tallish man of not very distinguished appearance with deeply fissured cheeks and fair receding hair: a sufferer from gastric disorders that kept him in what seemed to be unenterprising despondency. He had been, in fact, merely a quiet, reserved, conscientious man, and the most remarkable of his features were his very bright, remarkably clear blue eyes.

In each of the five dreams George was seeing his father off, but it was only in the fifth and last dream that any sort of conversation took place between them. Then, as his father leaned from the carriage window, they clasped hands and his father said:

'Good-bye, George. Awfully nice of you to see me off so late. Don't linger. It's pretty cold. The Midland Hotel at Skelby Moor will find me until Monday.'

Then, as the train began to move away and George turned to go too, a strange incident occurred. George almost ran into a hurrying figure of another man walking away from the train: a biggish, burly figure, healthily and expansively handsome, with a fine walnut brown moustache and an air of superlative confidence and engaging charm. This figure was expensively dressed in a thick grey ulster and a cocoa-brown bowler hat and was carrying a malacca cane umbrella and a rather shabby brown gladstone bag.

Nothing about all this would have been unusual except that the gladstone bag was, as George recognized, his father's. He had carried it on his travels for many years. In it he had brought home little presents for George as a boy, model railway engines, chocolate, toy soldiers, and so on, the sort of things that fathers love to bring their sons. It immediately occurred to George that the bag was being stolen from his father and he started shouting. When the figure in the ulster took no notice of this George started running, or rather trying to run. But as always in dreams his legs were incapable of moving and a second later he was awake, crying aloud, his heart racing.

Always, on waking, George could still smell the sulphurous tang of train smoke, the steamy odours of the restaurant car, the freezing bite of night air. The friendly depth of his father's voice – it was a remarkably coloured voice, a deep shade of brown – was so affectionately real in its every intonation that he fully expected to see him still sitting there at the bedside, still talking. The sudden shattering of the dream-world notion that his father was still alive left him first shocked and then sunk in unbearable loneliness. But what affected him even more deeply was the curious incident of the gladstone bag. Not only was the bag being stolen but somehow, because of it, George felt that a great wrong had been done to his father and it continued to haunt him like a pain.

At breakfast, after the fifth dream, he said: 'Is there such a place as Skelby Moor?'

'I don't know,' his mother said. Her answer seemed offhand. 'I never heard of it.'

His mother was a taut blonde woman of fifty with eyes so fair that they seemed to be lashless. She had an irritating breakfast habit of rapidly spreading butter on dry toast and then, in parsimonious thought, scraping most of it off again.

'Did father ever go there?'

'I don't think so. I never heard of it. Why are you asking?'

'I've got a funny idea I saw a post-card from there once.'

'Your father was always sending post-cards. He was the champion post-card sender.'

'I seem to remember something about fishing. Trout, I think, or it might have been salmon.'

'I don't suppose your father ever went fishing in his life,' she said. With irritation she did her toast scraping act for the second or third time. 'That would have been too enterprising.'

Looking away from him, she began to spread marmalade in a thin golden veneer on a square of toast.

'Do we still have the old post-card album?' he said. 'I mean the big brown one. The one with the brass clasps.'

'It's somewhere,' she said. 'I suppose it's somewhere.'

'I think I'll get it out.'

'Oh! don't go charging about!' she said. 'Don't go rummaging about upstairs.'

'I don't propose to go charging about,' he said. 'What is it about you this morning? What's up?'

'I've got a head. I'm brittle,' she said. 'I'm just brittle, that's all.'

'You've been brittle ever since father died.'

'And how else do you expect me to be?' she said. 'How else?'

After breakfast he started searching in a black tin trunk, up in the box-room, for the big post-card album with brass clasps that he remembered so often poring through as a boy. He supposed it had been started by his maternal grandmother. It began with views of Paris and the Promenade des Anglais at Nice, lemon trees at Mentone, heather-pink scenes of Scottish glens and portraits of famous people such as Houdini, Dan Leno, Caruso and Madame Patti. It ended with countless dutiful messages, meticulous and uninspired, from his father, the commercial traveller

in various lines of carpet slippers, from places as far apart as
Aberystwyth and Aberdeen. 'Weather not too good. Sold
ten gross to Watson & Watson today. Food at Wrexham
good. More peas than I could possibly eat. Not sure when I'll be
home.' It contained, among other things, a picture of his
mother when a young woman in an expensive-looking sleeveless afternoon dress with a skirt well above the knees. She looked
uncommonly attractive and vivacious. She was smiling and
her legs were very pretty. Unlike his father, his mother's side of
the family had been comfortably well off. They had travelled
a good deal: Nice and Mentone in the winter, Scotland in the
summer, Paris in the spring: so that she had rather grown up to
take pretty, expensive things for granted.

At the back end of the album there was a flap and in this he
found a loose assortment of about a dozen cards. On one of
these his father had written 'I've drawn you a picture of a fish
I caught yesterday. It weighed 2½ lbs and when they cooked it
for me at The Midland it was bright pink. Just like a shrimp.'
The little sketch of the fish had actually been drawn in red ink
and on the back was a picture of the parish church at Skelby
Moor.

The fact that the fish was sketched in red ink delighted him
and he at once supposed that this was why Skelby Moor had
lingered so long and so tenaciously in his memory. He went
downstairs excitedly, taking the card, and said:

'What do you make of that? Isn't that odd? There it is – the
fish and everything. In red ink. I remembered it from all that
time ago.'

'Very interesting.'

'These old albums are fun. I'm glad we kept it. By the way,
didn't we used to have another one?'

'Not to my knowledge. Not to my knowledge.'

'I feel sure we did. Can't you remember? I'm sure I used to
look at it as a boy.'

'Why all this sudden fuss about an album?' she said. 'Why
all this sudden cufuffle about Skelby Moor? You're not think-

ing of going there, are you? I thought you were going to Brighton in September.'

'I think I'm old enough to please myself where I go. There's no fuss.'

'Naturally. You're twenty-three.'

'As a matter of fact I am going. It's sort of got under my skin, this place. I've decided to go up for a long week-end.'

Suddenly, as he said this, some of her brittleness seemed to dissolve. A certain haggardness about the eyes was partially smoothed out. She seemed to become nervously alight and urged him quickly and almost too fussingly to let her pour him another cup of coffee.

'I think that's the way to do things. Quite impromptu. You always get the most fun when you do things at a tangent, don't you think? You could stay for a week if you wanted to. Why not?'

'I might if I can get the time.'

'Be sure to let me know when you're coming back though, won't you?'

He promised he would and then, five minutes later, started for the office, no longer haunted by the dream but feeling in a curious way uplifted. Skelby Moor, he told himself, might be fun. He might even catch himself a trout as pink and delectable as the one his father had sketched on the postcard.

Skelby Moor turned out to be a God-forsaken dingy little town of seven or eight thousand people on the edge of a coal-field in Derbyshire: a place of squat terraces half in red brick, half in grimy stone, with a short main street of shops, five or six pubs, two working men's clubs and an outdoor beerhouse or two. The square was of stone too, with a central market cross worn almost to alabaster smoothness by generations of lounging men.

Stone walls split the surrounding countryside of hills and dales into lopsided fragments, here and there mauve with heather, mostly bright green from summer rain. It was early

August when **he** arrived and the wind had a grizzling winter sound.

The Midland Hotel was also of stone, also grimy, and with a stout front portico. It stood close by the railway station. Trains shunted noisily past it all day and some part of the night, belching darkly. The navigation coal they used showered down a fine black dust that settled like a crowd of minute flies on window sills, table linen and even bedclothes.

The woman who kept the hotel, Mrs Lambton, was a stolid sort of cart mare. She had a well scrubbed appearance, almost over-clean. Her white blouse crackled.

'For how many nights would you want the room, sir?'

'I'm not sure. Four or five. Perhaps a week. I understand there's some good fishing here.'

'Oh?' she said. 'It's the first I heard of it.'

'Perhaps I've come to the wrong place after all,' he said. 'It's odd how – '

' Well, if you have you'd better book from night to night until you've made up your mind, hadn't you?'

'Let's say three nights,' he said. 'I'd like to do some walking anyway.'

He began to feel, from that moment, slightly foolish about it all. The long train journey – he had come by train in the slender hope that, in some sort of way, it might tell him something about that burly figure in the ulster – now seemed unnecessary and futile. The dream, though so consistently vivid and real in repetition, now started to mock him slightly.

After supper he walked about the town. From much rain the hills beyond it were acid green in the falling sunlight. In the distance, across the town, someone was practising scales on a cornet and soon the repeated monotonous phrases, like the dream, started to mock him too.

After half an hour of strolling about he went back to the hotel and ordered himself a beer. He stood at the bar, drinking it, and said to Mrs Lambton:

'I wonder if you remember my father? He used to stay here. Albert Pickard.'

She pondered for some moments, absently scratching one arm through the sleeve of her crackling blouse.

No, she told him at last, she'd never heard of anyone of that name. But then she wasn't so very good at names.

'Did he stay here often? When would this be? If he was a regular I'd remember him.'

'I think pretty often. I suppose he probably first came here seven or eight years ago. Probably longer.'

'Oh! that accounts for it,' she said. 'I wasn't here seven or eight years ago. My husband died suddenly and I got very run down what with one thing and another. You wouldn't per- haps believe it to look at me now, but I had a long bout of T.B. at that time. It nearly took me home.'

He sipped his beer, telling her that it really didn't matter. It was just that his father had mentioned the fishing at some time.

'My sister ran the place while I was away,' she said. 'I haven't been back so long.'

Suddenly, for some reason he couldn't explain, he felt in- tensely curious about the sister. Behind the hotel a train shunted past, belching smoke. A rattle of buffers hit the evening air, raising a chain of echoes that still hadn't died when he said:

'Is she here with you now?'

'Who, Kitty? No, I sent her away about a month ago,' she said. 'She was getting like me, a nervous wreck. I didn't like it. She'd been overworking a lot and got herself into a state. I sent her down to the sea for a while.'

'She'll be back, I suppose?'

'She'll be back next Friday, but whether she'll settle, I don't know – that's another matter. She's a restless girl, Kitty. Lately she's really got awfully restless. I sometimes wonder if she'll ever settle here any more.'

Perhaps it was the trains, he was on the point of saying. That constant battery of shunting trains raining black dust was hardly, he thought, a cure for restlessness. Instead he said:

'She's younger than you, I take it?'

'Oh! much. There's fifteen years between us. You'd never know us for sisters.'

Later in the evening he took another walk across the square. It was quite dark now and he could actually feel grains of smoke dust from the railway falling on his face and hair and hands. The air was dank with sulphur. This is a God-forsaken hole for a restless girl to live in, he thought, my God, how could you bear it? and from across the town, on the chilly August night wind, the monotonous scales of the cornet, still tenaciously playing, came to mock him in answer.

Three days later he was back home. It was late afternoon when he arrived. The front door of the house was locked and he noticed that the blinds of his mother's room were drawn. The afternoon had been rather showery, with only fitful bursts of sun, and it struck him at once that she shouldn't be at home.

After letting himself in with his latch-key he stood at the foot of the stairs and called up:

'Mother, are you there? Are you at home?'

There was no answer. He mounted three or four steps of the stairs and called again:

'Mother, I'm back. Are you in?'

This time, after a moment or two of silence, her voice, muffled from behind the bedroom door, answered:

'I'm lying down. I've had a terrible head all day. I've taken some aspirin and I'd like to be quiet for a while.'

'I'm sorry. Of course.'

'Get yourself some tea if you want some. If you wouldn't mind.'

'I won't bother,' he called. 'I'm right out of stamps and there are a few letters I want to do. I'll hop down to the post and get some and perhaps have a cup of tea at the Bun Shop on the way back.'

'Do that, dear. That's the simplest way.'

It was not until he was actually out of the door and into the street that his mind accepted the image of something he had seen while crossing the hall.

He hesitated for a moment, then let himself into the house again and stood for fully two minutes staring at a malacca cane umbrella hanging on the hat stand. The black cover was unrolled and slightly wet with rain.

With a strange feeling of not being himself, of being in some way disembodied, he started to walk slowly to the post office. Another shower was brewing, coming up from the west on blue-black clouds, and spots of rain were actually falling on his jacket without his noticing them when a voice hailed him:

'Hullo there, George. Back so soon?'

It was his boss, Freddy Rogers. In his engineering draughtsman's office they worked together more as colleagues than anything else. It wouldn't be long, Rogers promised, before they were partners.

'Why the swift return?'

'Didn't like the place. There was no fishing either.'

'You look a bit under par, old boy. Haven't been on the run, have you? You ought to get some sea air.'

'I'm off again the day after tomorrow,' he said. 'Taking the car this time. That's if it's all right with you.'

'Why don't you go to that little place on the Suffolk coast I told you about? It's terrifically bracing. It'll put any amount of ginger into you. You look as if you have bad dreams.'

'I sometimes do.'

'You've got to snap out of this, George,' Freddy said. 'We've got that big Smith & Hanson contract coming on in September.'

Back at the house he was writing letters in the sitting-room when his mother came downstairs, still in a dressing gown. She looked, he thought, rather more brittle than when he had left her three days before. Her eyes were unradiant and tired. She kissed him on both cheeks and said:

'Tell me about your holiday. Why are you back so soon?'

'It was too cold. I had all the wrong clothes with me. I'm off south the day after tomorrow, taking the car this time.'

'I'm glad about that. It's been cold and rainy here too.'

He licked the flap of an envelope, sealed it down and pressed it hard with the palm of his hand.

'By the way, whose umbrella was that I saw hanging in the hall? I don't remember seeing that before.'

With the utmost casualness she said:

'Is that your last letter? I'll walk to the post with them if you like. I feel I need some air.'

'I'm sorry. I forgot to ask how your head was.'

'It's a deal better. I took a fair bit of aspirin. The umbrella? It belonged to an insurance agent who called this afternoon. He forgot it. He came about the final settling up of your father's policy.'

'I thought it was already settled.'

'Well, so it is to all intents and purposes. It was just that they wanted another paper signed. It's an awful bore, the time they take to get things settled up. Not that it's a fat lump when it comes.'

'How much is it? I never asked you.'

'Three thousand.'

'It's something. You'll manage for a time.'

She started laughing with a peculiar distastefulness.

'Manage? Manage? I like to do more than manage in my life, thank you. I like nice things. I was brought up to like nice things. You can't expect me to live on bread and water.'

He made no answer to what he thought was an intolerable question. The eyes, behind their fair lashes, were becoming inflamed with temper. He had often seen them flame like that before.

'By the way, the umbrella isn't there now.'

'Oh! isn't it? How odd. It couldn't be, I suppose, because he came back and fetched it five minutes ago?'

Again he made no answer. She moved towards the door,

brittle again in her every movement, hands forming a restless cage as she locked them in front of her.

'Is there any great urgency about the letters?' she said. 'If not, I'll get some supper and take them later.'

'No. No urgency. Just when you feel you'd like to go.'

'All right.' She was already out of the room. 'They'll go at midnight anyway.'

After supper, tired out and once again oppressed by the curious feeling of being disembodied, not quite himself, he went to bed, leaving his mother to post the letters. The night was very quiet. It seemed suddenly to have grown quite sultry and he lay for a long time with eyes open, re-living among other things the sound of the cornet being practised, the scales haunting and mocking him like the dream of his father.

When he finally slept he was woken some long time later by two sounds: the shriek of a train roaring through the night and the sound of his mother coming home.

As she started to climb the stairs he switched on his torch and looked at his watch.

It was half past two.

By Saturday he was back in Skelby Moor. The spell of wintry August rain had given way first to sultriness, then to clear brilliant sunshine. Everywhere the green hills were alight, fresh and sparkling.

As he walked into the silent and empty lobby of The Midland Hotel he suddenly realized, too late, that half past three in the afternoon is not the best of all possible times at which to arrive at small provincial hotels. The staff are generally resting; the proprietress is either out walking or asleep in her room; the boots is having forty winks or waiting for the racing results or playing cards.

After banging twice without result on a big bell that stood on the reception counter he went and sat in a big horse-hair chair in the lounge. He started to read a magazine in which there was a great deal about dogs and horses. Both were animals in which he hadn't the slightest interest and suddenly he felt his eyes begin to close.

Some time later, half asleep, he began to have the strangest feeling that he was being stared at. He also actually thought he heard a voice say 'Oh! Good God,' in an astonished half whisper.

He opened his eyes and looked up to see, standing in the doorway of the lounge, a woman of twenty-nine or so with thick attractive dark hair and large enveloping brown eyes. There was a certain restless air of shyness about her that was, as he afterwards discovered, almost entirely the result of sheer surprise. Her dress was pure white linen with scarlet pipings on the cuffs and collar and it looked as if it had just been ironed.

He knew, somehow, that this was Mrs Lambton's sister. She in turn looked at him as if about to greet him with some exclamatory form of recognition. She had the air of being suddenly confronted by a familiar face she hadn't seen for some time.

'I'm sorry. Did you want something? Have you been waiting long?'

'Not really.' He got up from the chair. 'No hurry. It doesn't matter.'

'Did you ring? I was upstairs changing my dress. I didn't hear the bell.'

'It really didn't matter – '

'Was it a room you wanted?'

'Yes. Just for three or four days.'

'Of course. Perhaps you would register?'

Her voice was warm, quiet and inclined to be rather slow. The vowels, in the northern way, were a little high but altogether without a trace of sharpness.

At the reception desk she turned the visitors book round to him so that he could fill in his name. He was unscrewing the top of his fountain-pen when, to his own intense surprise, she said:

'It is Mr Clarkson, isn't it?'

When he said no, he was sorry, it wasn't Mr Clarkson, her face suddenly flushed very deeply and then, within some seconds, went dead white, not merely startled but completely shocked.

'Oh! really? I felt sure I recognized you. I felt sure you must have stayed with us here before. I'm so sorry. Your face seemed so –'

She made a flurried pretence of searching about the desk for papers. Her hands were nervous, slender and pale. There was no ring on them and he said:

'As a matter of fact I have. I was here a few days ago. Mrs Lambton made me very comfortable.'

'Oh! yes, my sister. She's out this afternoon.' He was writing his name in the book now. 'My eldest brother came to fetch her for a drive. They're going to have tea somewhere –'

He had finished writing his name by now. He turned the book round towards her and she looked at it and said:

'Oh! I see. Mr Pickard? I do hope you didn't think it stupid of me just now, Mr Pickard? I really did think –'

Not all the nervousness had quite gone out of her voice and eyes and hands and he tried to reduce the situation to final calmness by saying:

'It's just one of those things that could happen to anybody. After all I might say that I'd seen you before. You're quite like your sister.'

'Oh! you really think so? Hardly anybody does.'

'I think so.'

'Perhaps in looks a little,' she said, 'but not in temperament. Certainly not in temperament.'

As if this were meant to put a sudden stop to the conversation about her she turned abruptly and took the key of room No. 12 from a rack behind her.

'I had No. 7 last time,' George Pickard said. 'It was very quiet –'

'I'm afraid there's a gentleman in there now. He may be out by Monday. But No. 12 is quite nice. It really is –'

'Of course. It was only that the trains – '

'Oh! the trains won't disturb you in No. 12.'

As she took him upstairs to No. 12 he half paused on the landing and said:

'Oh! there was something I wanted to ask you. I understand there's some decent fishing here.'

'Not here,' she said. 'Not exactly here. But four or five miles up the dale there's a place. Quite a nice stream – '

'Does one need permission?'

'Oh! you simply take a daily ticket, I think. That's what – '

She broke off, again with that sudden intimation of the conversation being closed. A moment later she had unlocked the door of No. 12 and he was in the room, gazing again at the familiar swarm of coal dust on window sills, furniture and even counterpane.

'You must tell me when you want to go,' she said, 'and I'll give you directions.'

'I'll probably go tomorrow,' he said. 'I'll take advantage of the weather. It's a good spell.'

She lingered at the door, ready but reluctant to close it. She looked altogether calmer now. The deep, good-looking brown eyes were not troubled. The embarrassment of having mistaken him for someone else had been replaced by an air of rumination.

'I envy you going there,' she said. 'I like that place. I really envy you.'

After that she seemed to disappear from the hotel completely. It was Mrs Lambton who served drinks when the bar opened and again Mrs Lambton who came to ask the guests, at dinner, if all was well. Mrs Lambton was cheerful, glad to see everybody, glad to be of service and even reminded George Pickard to tell the night porter exactly what he wanted for breakfast and when. They believed in good breakfasts at The Midland and there were some lovely kippers.

After dinner, as before, he wandered into the square. Trains shunted smokily about in the sultry August twilight. What a place for a restless girl to be caught up in, he thought again, and once more started instinctively listening for the cornet's mournful, mocking scales.

But this time there was no sound of them and as the light finally faded he started to walk back to the hotel. A figure in a white dress but now with a scarlet sweater slung loosely over the shoulders stood under the big stone portico and a voice said:

'Admiring our great metropolis?'

He laughed briefly.

'It isn't so bad when it's dark.'

'I often think that,' she said. 'I often think it's a mercy we have nights.'

'The night is merciful – didn't someone once say that somewhere?'

'I don't know. If they didn't they should have done.'

A moment later he was about to ask her if she would join him in a drink when she said:

'I hope you won't mind but there was something I wanted to ask you. Or rather show you.'

'Oh! Yes?'

'Walk along the street a little way with me, will you?' she said. 'Just away from the hotel?'

It was now obvious to him that she was having the greatest difficulty in keeping calm. Several times, in spite of the sultry evening, she nervously hitched her sweater more closely round her shoulders.

Fifty yards away, at the corner of the square, a street lamp was burning. She stopped under it, unfastened her handbag and took out a post-card.

'I just wondered if this might mean anything to you. Of course I don't really suppose it does, but if – '

He took the card and stared at it under the street lamp. It was a picture of his father.

'Does it? Do you know that man?'

He stood for some time staring at the card, unsure himself now, not knowing what to say.

'If you do please tell me.'

He gave the card back to her. He was sharply aware of a bitter sickness contracting the back of his throat.

'Yes,' he said at last. 'It's my father.'

She stood against the lamp-post, gripping it with one hand exactly as if in fear that she hadn't the strength to stand up by herself.

'Can you tell me something else? Where is he now?'

'He's dead. He – '

'What?'

The word sounded like a stifled scream; she actually stood with one hand clapped to her mouth, face dead white under the lamp.

'He died six weeks ago.'

She made a sudden sharp and helpless movement so that for a moment he felt sure that she was falling. Instead she merely turned and held blindly, with both hands, to the street lamp.

'Oh! my God,' was all she kept saying. 'Oh! my God. My dear God.'


No rain had freshened the narrow stream for some days and now the water, in most places, was low and clear. It spilled with leaping brilliance past limestone boulders stained apple-green at the water line and between banks of birch, thick bracken and occasional larch trees. It was the hottest Sunday of the year, George Pickard thought, and in places where big pools formed under trees the water lay in undisturbed glassy darknesses.

'I still think I shouldn't have come,' she said. 'I know how fishermen like to be alone.'

'I asked you to come.'

'Being asked isn't necessarily a reason for – '

'I asked you to come.'

He had asked her to come because she was, he thought, in no state to be alone and now they were sitting, half-way through the sultry afternoon, by one of the deeper glassy pools. She was wearing a dress that he liked very much: a fresh, simple affair of printed cotton, with a pattern of crimson rose-buds, a rather flared skirt and a low circular neck-line. She looked rather younger than on the previous day, he thought, and though for long periods she was very quiet she seemed altogether less taut, less nervous and with no trace of hesitation.

In the bracken a prolonged chorus of grasshoppers had the effect of filling the long silences between conversation with a quivering tension. His fishing-rod lay undone in its canvas case on the bank; not a single hint of a rise had so far marked the dark skin of water. In one of the longer silences she took off her shoes and then lay full-length on the grass, slowly and exquisitely flexing her bare white feet.

'How did you come to know about Skelby Moor in the first place? I suppose your father must have told you?'

It began with a post-card, he started to tell her – his father had drawn a picture of a fish on a post-card – and then a dream.

'A dream?'

He half-started to tell her about the dream and then stopped. The strangest of all the effects that the long spells of tension between them produced was a feeling of growing remoteness from each other. He wanted all the time to get to know her better; all the time he felt she was slipping farther away.

'Don't you want to tell me anything about the dream?'

'Not at the moment.'

The words seemed to take him still farther away from her. He heard one of her feet lapping quietly at the surface of the pool. He sat looking at her, in silence, for a long time, noticing how pretty her head was when she held it to one side, watching her feet and the water. The face looked wonderfully cool, he thought, in the warm shadows.

'What exactly made you come up here anyway?' she said at last. 'I mean to Skelby Moor. To that awful place. Nobody in their right senses would come up here for a holiday.'

He thought for some moments in silence and then said:

'Have you ever come to a street corner and felt you simply

had to turn it even though it wasn't the way you intended going?'

'Often.'

'It was like that.'

How else could he explain, he asked himself, what had made him come up there? There were things that were never capable of rational explanation and he was suddenly aware of juggling confusedly with half-truths, and again of not being himself, of not knowing where he was.

'Have you had the dream again since you came up here?'

'No. Why?'

For the first time she gave a little laugh, quite happily.

'Just curiosity. I wondered if I might have been in it, that's all.'

He was about to say that he wished she had when she went on:

'Do dreams fascinate you?'

'This one does.'

'They fascinate me terribly. I dreamed one night that I was walking about bare-foot in the snow, looking for the key of our old house, the one where I was born. Then another night I dreamed I was the wife of a sort of tax collector in Persia, in the year 400 B.C. You see, you couldn't know it was 400 B.C., could you, in the first place? How do you explain dreams of that sort?'

He hadn't the faintest idea, he said, any more than he could explain this one.

'There's a strange line I remember about dreams. I read it in a poem at school. It stuck in my mind.' She lifted her right foot from the water. Something about its pure whiteness, dripping clear beads of water in the shadow, pricked sharply at his veins, making the blood start racing. ' "Thou art so truth that thoughts of thee suffice to make dreams truth; and fables histories." Do you know that?'

No, he didn't know that, he said. It was very beautiful but he had never heard it before. He was really watching the naked curve of her leg, uplifted from the water. It was pretty and smooth and elegant and again he felt his blood start racing.

Suddenly he thought: 'Was it a dream that made you call me Clarkson yesterday?' and the words were out of his mouth before he could stop them.

'It was just a silly mistake. It was just one of those odd things –'

'Tell me the truth,' he said, 'will you?'

She turned at once and transfixed him with her wide deep brown eyes and half extended a hand as if about to touch him.

'Get to know me a little better first,' she said. 'Please.'

'How do I get to know you better?' He turned impulsively and pressed his mouth lightly against her throat. He could feel it throbbing quickly and he drew back and said 'Like this?'

'If you like. Whichever way you like. You see I've been through a bad time and –'

Suddenly she put her arms round his neck in a gesture of intolerable longing. He started to kiss her but with a twisted movement, almost in anguish, she broke away.

'Tell me what made you come up here,' she said. 'Please.'

'I've tried to tell you –'

'How did you know about me? Did your father ever say anything to you about me?'

No, he said, not once. His father had never said a word.

'But how on earth could you know? – I mean – how on earth, that's what I keep asking.'

He ran his hands slowly across her bare shoulders. The first fish of the afternoon rose with a sharp plop in the centre of the pool, startling her. 'What was that?' she said and he caressed her slowly again, trying to calm her, this time smoothing the downy hair in the nape of her neck.

'You were fond of my father, weren't you?' he said.

'Yes.'

'Very fond?'

'Very fond. In fact you could call it more than that.'

He was holding her face in his hands now, turning it fully towards him.

'Was he fond of you?'

'In a sort of way. Yes.'

'In a sort of way?'

'Yes. I can't explain now. I've told you I'd rather not talk about it now.'

He was looking full into her face, full into the deep brown eyes, troubled again now.

'You ask me to get to know you better,' he said, 'and all the time you go farther away.'

'Oh! don't look at me like that,' she said. 'That's cruel. Don't you know how like your father you are in some ways? You've got those same clear blue eyes. Don't you see that's why I made that mistake about you yesterday?'

A moment later she flung her arms impulsively about him again and he drew her down in the grass. He ran his hands from her neck to her shoulders and down to her arms and then finally across her breasts, firm and free under the thin cotton frock. In return she kissed him with searching passion, without a word, for a long time, the chorus of grasshoppers beating without rest, in a prolonged throbbing murmur, through the hot afternoon.

Clarkson, his mind kept repeating, Clarkson. Why did she call me Clarkson? Who the devil can Clarkson be? Caught up between passion, the tender feel of her breasts under his hands and the old confusion about half-truths, he found his mind full of the most mocking surmises.

Was that Clarkson with that blasted umbrella? Could that have been Clarkson boarding the train?

After that it began to seem strange and uneasy to speak of his father. By the end of the hot restless afternoon he had become merely an embarrassing ghost, thrust away into the background, half-forgotten. Incredibly it seemed that she actually wanted to forget him and it was some days before he was back in the conversation. And then inconsequentially she said:

'What sort of woman is your mother?'

'Oh! I don't know. Fairly ordinary, I suppose.'

'Nobody is fairly ordinary.'

'Well, she's got a devil of a difficult temper sometimes. She has days.'

It was shortly past eleven o'clock in the morning. She was doing her turn of duty in the bar. George Pickard, drinking beer, was her only customer. She herself, as she had several times explained, never drank on duty.

But suddenly, to his great surprise, she started to pour herself a double whisky, saying at the same time:

'I'm going to take you up on that drink you're always offering me. Hope you don't mind?'

'Please,' he said. 'Of course. But why the sudden change of heart?'

She drank, stared for some time into the glass, drank again and finally looked up at him.

'I suppose it would shock you awfully if I said I loathed and hated your mother?'

It shocked him so much that he was completely without a word of any kind to say.

'I thought you'd be shocked. I'm sorry. But I've got to get it off my chest some time.'

'But you've never met my mother.'

'That makes no difference.'

As he watched her drinking it seemed to him once again that they were playing with half-truths: and this time dangerously.

'Look,' he said, 'you'd better tell me about this. You've been putting it off too long.'

'Not now. Tonight.'

'Why tonight?'

A moment later she reminded him of his remark about the night being merciful. She felt all mixed up now, she said, and she would find it easier to talk in the dark.

'You could come into my room,' she said. 'I'll tell you about it then.'

It was almost midnight before he went into her room. The

night was another close, sultry one and she lay in her night-gown on the bed, waiting.

It was nearly another hour before she started talking. She talked with her mouth close to his face, in a continuous whisper that at first he hardly ever interrupted. First of all she must tell him, she said, why she had called him Clarkson. It was simply that that was the name she'd always known his father by; she never knew him by any other. She was not much more than twenty-two when Mr Clarkson, the traveller in slippers, first booked a room one very cold night in November. She always remembered it vividly because, ashen and half crippled with cold and dyspepsia, he had asked for a glass of peppermint and hot water. After that he began to come to the hotel regularly: about once a month, she thought. In the usual way with regular guests she got to know him quite well. They chatted in an ordinary sort of way in the lounge or the bar. He was quiet, gentle, unassuming and unvindictive, a really nice man, and she felt sorry for him because he seemed lonely and be-cause of the stomach pains.

'Why on earth do you suppose he should tell you his name was Clarkson?'

She'd never asked herself, she said. At that time she hadn't any need. Anyway it all went on in that ordinary sort of way until about a year later. Then on another cold wet night he walked in with his bags from the station, half-exhausted, and started drinking good and hard.

'But my father never drank,' he said. 'He never touched it.'

She was afraid he did, she said, and that night especially. The barman actually refused to serve him in the end and then, about eleven o'clock, as she herself went up to bed, she stopped on the landing because she could hear a strange sound from No. 7. It was the sound of his father, bitterly weeping. If there was one sound in the world that made her heart bleed, she said, it was the sound of a grown man crying like that. And that night it upset and haunted her so much that she didn't sleep for more than an hour or so. She had one of those horrible white nights, she said, when the mind ranges starkly, or dreams badly, making sleep a mockery.

'It was that night I dreamed I was wandering bare-foot in the snow,' she said, 'trying to find the key of our old house.'

Next day she felt terribly on edge and restless, half exhausted herself now, and she knew, somehow, that she had to ask him about it. By an unexpected chance he came in extra early for lunch that day and she was alone in the bar, doing her turn of duty. Over a glass of steaming peppermint he began slowly to tell her all about it: how he had gone home unexpectedly, a week before, and had found Mrs Clarkson – no, of course it would be Mrs Pickard – busily entertaining a man friend upstairs. It wasn't exactly this circumstance itself that grieved him so much; it was the fact that it had happened before.

The first occasion, it seemed, had had a good deal of publicity. It had been pretty awful, it seemed. His father had beaten the man up badly, quite savagely in fact, inflicting shocking injuries with a walking stick; he sort of went berserk and there was a prosecution. The man came from rather a wealthy family, who briefed a crack counsel, and his father was finally found guilty of causing grievous bodily harm and sentenced, she thought, to two months in gaol. It was the prison sentence, coupled with the worry, the misery and the utter humiliation of it all, that first started those awful dyspeptic attacks that finally dragged him down.

In absolute astonishment he managed to say: 'But I can't believe it. I never missed my father at any time.'

'It happened when you were away at boarding-school,' she said. 'They kept it from you. It was a winter term. He told me that. It was the thing that nearly drove him mad, of course – the idea that you might get to know somehow and it would be a terrible stigma on you and so on. And then his own awful shame.'

'That was why he called himself Clarkson when he took the traveller's job,' he said. 'I remember him taking that job now. He used to be top man in a rather good gentlemen's outfitters and then all of a sudden he had this new job, travelling about the country.'

Suddenly her voice stopped being merely warm and reflective. It flared up, dry with anger..

'I suppose you know he adored your mother? Adored and absolutely worshipped her? He carried pictures of her about with him. That was why he forgave her and went back to her – and you, of course. He had to think of you. That was what made it such hell. He was terribly fond of you too.'

'I was terribly fond of him,' he said. And then, inconsequentially too, he found himself with a strange question to ask: 'Did my father ever make love to you?'

'No,' she said, 'I wanted him to. Very much. I even suggested it. But it wasn't that sort of love he wanted. He didn't want it that way.'

She supposed, she went on to say, that it was really that refusal of his that was responsible for her own affection for him continually getting stronger and stronger.

'You see it wasn't me he wanted. It was your mother – always, all the time. I was just someone he was fond of and could talk to. And after a time – it was a long time too and I was very young – I realized that's all I ever would be. And then it started being hell for me too.'

After that he kissed her for a time and then asked her if she were sleepy. No, she wasn't sleepy, she said; she wanted to talk some more.

'Let me talk for a bit,' he said. 'I want to ask you one or two more things. About that second time – the time my father found a man in the house. Was it the same man?'

'It was,' she said. 'That was the bitter part of it.'

'I suppose he never told you what sort of man he looked like? Did he ever describe him at all?'

'He called him a handsome bastard. I remember that. He had the money to dress well too. And to spend on your mother. Your father was very bitter about that.'

He lay for some time in silence, ruminating, his mouth against her cheek, and then said:

'That dream I told you about. There was a man in that.'

'Yes?'

'He was a handsome bastard too.' Slowly he told her of the ulster, the malacca cane umbrella, the bowler hat, the brown handsome moustache. 'How the hell does he come to be in this dream? I've never seen him in my life before.'

'I suppose you could have seen a picture in the paper at the time of the case.'

'We weren't allowed daily papers at school. I don't know if it's the same man anyway.'

In a whisper he could hardly hear she said it was all very strange: just as strange as her own dreams about Persia and wandering in the snow and the way he himself knew there was a place called Skelby Moor and a Midland Hotel there. There was no knowing how the mind worked; there was no rational way of explaining these things.

'The Skelby Moor part isn't so strange,' he told her. 'I already told you. I found that post-card about it in an old album. My father had drawn a fish on it, in red. I suppose it was the fish that made it stick in my mind.'

A recollection of the album took his thoughts back home. He started to think of the other album, the one he could only half remember. He recalled how greatly irritated his mother had been at the mention of it. He remembered her sarcastic impatience at his mention of Skelby Moor, her confession about her morning brittleness.

A few moments later a night goods express ran through the station, whistling as it passed. The reflected glow from the fire-box came up through a slit in the window blind and slid slowly across the ceiling like a crimson bar.

Some time after the sound of the train had passed completely into the distance he said suddenly:

'Good God, I've just remembered something.'

'About your father?'

'No: about my mother.'

For the second time a recollected incident of his boyhood sprang as sharply across his mind as the reflection of the fire-box across the ceiling.

'I've just remembered a day when she threatened to thrash me within an inch of my life.'

For fully a minute of astonished silence he propped himself up on one elbow, staring down at her naked body, hardly believing what he had remembered.

'I'd been playing tennis,' he said. 'It came on to rain and we gave it up and I went back home. My mother was out somewhere. I was disappointed about the tennis and I was bored with having nothing to do. I started wandering about the house, poking into drawers and cupboards. We had a linen cupboard on the stairs and I found another album in it, hidden under a pile of sheets – one I hadn't seen before. It was covered in bright red suède.'

He remembered that album with great vividness now. It was full of photographs: one to a page. He remembered taking it downstairs, spreading it on the kitchen table and turning over the thick cardboard leaves.

He remembered too his mother coming home.

' Why are you always meddling with things? The way you behave sometimes is enough to make a saint swear.' She was shouting in the most brittle, livid of voices. 'Keep your hands off my property. Do you hear? Keep your hands off my property. I'll thrash you within an inch of your life if it happens again. Do you hear?'

He felt sweat breaking out all over his body at the recollection of the scene. Half exhausted, he lay down in the bed, his head against her bare shoulder.

'That was where I saw him first,' he said. 'There were seven or eight pictures of him and he'd scrawled across every one of them. Good God, why didn't I remember it before?'

Sometimes the mind had a funny way of covering up unpleasant things, she said. Sort of putting a callus over them. Healing the sore.

'His name was Harry,' he said. 'I remember now. He'd scrawled on every damn picture. "To my sweetest darling Babs, with everlasting love, Harry." '

'There was a place your father liked very much to go to,' she said next morning. 'It's high up. You can see across several counties on a clear day. I'd like to take you there.'

They drove up, that afternoon, to a treeless hill of almost sugar-loaf shape high above the dales. Among white limestone crags the dry turf was as short and fine as if pared off with a razor; harebells in blue crowds fluttered about it in a light wind like delicately suspended fragile butterflies. In the low nearer distances patches of heather stained the slopes a peculiar smoky shade of red.

'He always loved to come up here,' she said, 'even in winter. He said it made him feel released from something – I suppose sort of free.'

The breeze, even at that height, was quite warm and after looking down at the immense wide view for a few moments he took off his jacket and spread it over a rock. She sat down and leaned her back against it and he sat with her, one arm across her shoulders.

'He said an awful thing to me just before we came up here for the first time,' she said. 'It was the thing that really made my heart start breaking for him. He said, "I feel as if my soul's all locked up in chains." It was a terrible thing for a man to say and I never got over it. I never got it out of my mind.'

Suddenly his heart started aching for his father; he was aware of being uncomfortably close to him again. The lean fissured figure, struggling against pain, took on a new and biting reality.

'It put my soul in chains too,' she said, 'and then I don't know quite what made me think of it but one afternoon I suggested we took a bus and came up here. He loved it. For the first time I actually realized he was happy. His eyes even started dancing.'

He felt utterly unable to speak. He was abruptly aware that if he didn't force himself into some sort of sudden physical action his eyes would fill with tears. Without a word he got up and walked away from her and stood for nearly ten minutes on the edge of the hillside, staring blindly down.

'Sorry,' he said. Back with her again, he sat down and she briefly gripped his hands.

'Don't do that again,' she said. 'I know how you feel but please don't do it again. Everything you did then was exactly like him. You looked so terribly lonely. It might have been him standing there.'

'I missed him like hell when it first happened,' he said. 'I suppose that's why I dreamed so much about him. Now somehow I've started to miss him more and more.'

For the next few moments he was so imprisoned by the blinding reality of his own emotions that he almost forgot that she was there. He finally found himself staring at her in stupefied astonishment. Her face was buried in her hands.

He started bitterly to reproach himself and begged her not to cry but she went on crying, almost silently, for some minutes longer. When it was all over she sat biting her knuckles and in a double rush of affection for herself and his father he sat helplessly wondering what to say.

'There was something I wanted to ask you,' she said at last.

'Yes?'

'How much longer are you staying here?'

'I've got to go back home,' he said. 'I've got to see my mother.'

'Do you have to go?'

Uncontrollably all his emotions suddenly broke in a bitter rush of fury against his mother: the vain, brittle toast-scraper, the darling Babs, the lover of pretty things.

'Good Jesus Almighty,' he half shouted, 'don't you understand? She even sits there waiting for the damned insurance!

She killed him – she and that bastard – and she sits there calmly waiting to collect the blood money – '

He was pacing up and down across the short grass now, hair blowing untidily in the wind, one fist beating into the palm of the other hand.

'I've got to get back there today,' he said. 'There's a million things I've got to say.'

She had sense enough not to try to check or pacify him and for some minutes he continued to rage up and down. Finally, when he appeared a little calmer, she said:

'Will you be coming back?'

'Yes, I'll be coming back.'

As if a sluice had been opened all his rage suddenly poured clean away; he simply stood there gazing into the thoughtful, troubled brown eyes, holding her face in his hands.

'I'll be back late tomorrow. Have your bag packed.'

'My bag packed?'

'Yes,' he said. 'You're going to marry me, aren't you? I hope you will, Kitty. I'm asking you.'

With a little cry, but not speaking, she started laughing for the first time that day.

'Mind you're waiting,' he said, laughing too. 'Be here.'

'I'll be waiting,' she said.


It was already dark when he arrived home that evening but the light in the sitting-room was still burning. He had stopped at The Cartwright Arms farther down the street to book himself a room for the night and get himself a double whisky for his nerves, but when he went into the sitting-room he was still tense and trembling.

His mother was sitting by an electric fire, reading a magazine. It was raining outside and he didn't even bother to unbutton his mackintosh.

'You're back. Why didn't you let me know you were coming?'

'I just dropped in for some things. I'm going straight back.'
He put his hat on the table. 'I'm going to be married.'

'Nice of you to tell me.'

With extreme difficulty he kept his voice terse, even restrained.

'Surprised you're alone,' he said. 'No company? Where's Harry?'

'Harry?'

'Yes, Harry. Don't tell me you don't know our Harry.'

If he had struck her full in the face she couldn't have looked more stunned. For fully a minute she continued to sit in the chair and then slowly she got up, dropping the magazine in a noisy slide.

'As it interests you so much, I haven't seen Harry since your father died.'

'How Harry must miss you.'

'And nor, since it still seems to interest you so much, shall I be seeing him again. Quite satisfied?'

'Don't tell me Harry's dead too.'

If anything was dead, he thought, it was her face. It had never been, he thought, a very soft or ardent face. Vanity had always given it, with those extremely fair lashes, a veneer of superficiality. Now it was white and, like an old skeletonized leaf, almost transparent too.

'Harry got married,' she said.

'I hope you congratulated him.'

'His mother died and left him an awful lot of money. He got married almost immediately. He's got a house in Cannes.'

Her voice, like her face, seemed skeletonized and lifeless too. Still tense and bitter, he was about to make some remark in the most cynical possible manner about how it was all rather a bad stroke of luck for her when she said, in the flattest of voices:

'It was almost directly after your father died. You don't know Harry, do you? Harry's the sort of man who gets a great kick out of having other men's wives while their husbands are alive. When the husbands are dead it's all too tame. Not fun any more.'

He made no attempt to match her bitterness with a renewal of his own until a sudden thought struck him.

'I don't believe it,' he said. 'He was here last week. Wasn't that his damned umbrella hanging up in the hall?'

'I told you the truth about the umbrella. Anyone can have an umbrella like that. Anyone can leave an umbrella by mistake, can't they? It was the insurance man's.'

'Ah! the insurance,' he said. 'We come to the insurance.' He could control himself no longer; all his rage boiled over in a hot stream of shouts. 'You killed him, you and that bastard. Oh! I don't mean you poisoned him or anything so bloody simple as that. You didn't hit him over the head with a wrench. But you killed him just the same. He died of an overdose of shame, poor devil. And now you sit waiting for the insurance. Oh! I like the insurance part very much. Very much. It's bloody funny.'

He picked up his hat from the table.

'So you haven't seen him?' he said. Once more the main stream of his rage had drained suddenly away. 'What about the night you didn't come back until half past two?'

'I was just walking.'

'Of course. Naturally. With the great Harry.'

He was on the verge of shouting at her something about being a damn bad liar too when she said:

'Yes, just walking. By myself. All alone.'

Her face, he thought, looked older than ever. It was even more a skeleton of a face than before. Pity for her suddenly fused with all his blinding affection for his father and kept him speechless. He heard her say:

'I haven't had anyone to turn to. I thought perhaps you'd help me a bit. I need some help. I'm almost in despair –'

He changed his name! his mind started shouting. He was ashamed of his own name. He went creeping about the country like a stranger, afraid of being recognized.

'I can't help you!' he shouted. It was all over. He felt empty and old himself now. 'I've nothing left to help you with.'

Early next day he drove northwards under moist humid clouds that gave occasional showers of drizzle. Half way to Skelby Moor he decided, on a sudden impulse, to stop and buy his wedding present to Kitty. He thought that one of those beauty boxes, with internal fittings of brushes, powder-puffs, mirrors, and so on, would be the very thing.

He stopped at the next town and found a shop and eventually picked out what he thought was a neat, stylish box in scarlet leather. As the shop assistant was making out his bill he suddenly found himself saying:

'I don't suppose you've got such a thing as a post-card album, have you?'

'No, sir, I'm afraid not. There's no call for them now. We never stock them. They seem to be out of fashion now.'

'I see. Thank you. I just wondered.'

He paid the bill and picked up the beauty box.

'They were good fun, those old albums, weren't they?' the assistant said. 'Don't you think so?'

'Great fun,' he said. 'Awful fun.'

He drove northwards again. Soon in the distance the hills began to rise through the drizzle and as he drove on, thinking more and more of Kitty, he watched them: slowly appearing and then suddenly disappearing, almost mysteriously, in the drifting summer cloud, like creatures in a dream.

'Be there,' he kept saying to himself. He seemed to see her lying once again in the bed, with the crimson bar of light travelling across the ceiling above her. 'Be waiting.' He seemed to see also his mother's face, old and skeletonized by its own despair. 'And for God's sake be true to me.'

# The Quiet Girl

When Maisie Foster was a child her mother sent her to one of those Edwardian villa private day schools where, for a few guineas a term, she could be sure of a kind of exclusive but wholly inadequate education that commoner children were denied. Other girls might rampage happily about the streets, spinning-tops, skipping, playing hop-scotch, or even having fun with boys, but those things were not for Maisie. Much of the useless curriculum was undoubtedly concerned with decorum, but it is equally certain that Maisie learned there two of the most important things in her life: sewing and the art of isolation. She was what everyone would have called a quiet girl.

At seventeen she left school and, since sewing was her chief accomplishment, went to work for a dressmaker named Miss Parsons, who had a small establishment of the customer's-own-material-made-up type behind the churchyard. The short back street there was made up mostly of solicitors' offices in Georgian buildings with black front doors, two doctors' houses, an estate agent's and an auctioneer's: a quiet street very much in keeping with her nature.

Half-way along the street a narrow stone-paved alleyway branched off and here Miss Parsons lived on two floors: work-rooms below and modest living quarters above. Miss Parsons was sixty, papery of appearance and short of breath; she had been warned of the dangers of stairs. Dressmakers, owing probably to the nature of their work, often tend to seem delicate, even meticulous of movement; but this was never true of Maisie. In spite of her quietness she seemed very much like a strongly coiled spring. It seemed likely that some day something or someone would touch her and she would respond like a rampant charge of electricity. All this was belied by an undistinctive appearance: her face was soft, rather dripping-coloured and never really quite healthy in appearance; the skin seemed slightly greasy and the dark hair never quite adequately brushed up; her brown eyes had that downy appearance seen on moth wings.

She was the sort of a girl that men are popularly supposed never to look at twice, but she belonged also to the category of women who, unblessed with good looks, nevertheless have excellent figures. She was generously formed but compact, rather large in the hips but on the whole very well-proportioned.

Five years after she had joined Miss Parsons she one day heard a short cry and a thumping sound from upstairs and ran there to find Miss Parsons face downwards on the top step, struck down by a sudden heart attack. In two days she was dead.

Maisie was now twenty-two and living with her mother and her father's sister on the far side of the town. Her father, a clerk to a firm of leather factors, had been dead ten years or more. Presently, in her quiet way, she was going home to tell her mother:

'Miss Parsons left a codicil to her will saying that if I wish I can take over the lease and the business without having to pay anything for the goodwill. I think I shall take it. It was very generous of her. It seems the opportunity of a lifetime.'

Her mother agreed that it was. ' Will you go there to live?' she said, 'or will you carry on here with us?'

'I shall go there, I think,' she said. 'I'd really like to start out on my own.'

Within a week she retired into the dressmaking establishment quietly and unobtrusively, as into a shell. Customers continued to bring in their own materials, to ponder over pattern books, to take fittings and chat about the weather.

The order books were nearly always full; in her quiet way she worked industriously.

One afternoon a woman of twenty-six or so, just engaged to be married, came in to ask if Maisie could perhaps find her a material of rather a special colour. It was to match the turquoise ring she was wearing – not quite the blue of a thrush's egg and not quite that of a forget-me-not. A very difficult blue, but one she had set her heart on.

In the square in front of the church there were ten or a dozen shops of the sort you always find in small country towns: a grocer's, a pork-butcher's, a seed-shop, a tea room, and so on. The biggest of these, with a fairly large double front, was a draper's owned by a man named Ashley Walpole. Maisie occasionally went to the shop for odd materials, buttons, cottons, accessories, and so on.

Later that afternoon she crossed the square, went into the shop and began to describe the particular blue colour to the chief assistant, a Mrs Fitzgerald, who went up to London once or twice a month on buying missions, often for special orders. Once again the particular shade of blue proved to be a very difficult one to define.

'It isn't exactly a thrush-egg blue,' Maisie was saying, 'perhaps it's nearer that vitriol blue – you know, a sort of chemical blue.'

As she and Mrs Fitzgerald were discussing this, but without much success, a voice behind her said:

'Some difficulty, Miss Foster? Something I can do to help?'

It was Ashley Walpole himself: a man of forty, tallish, unspontaneous of movement, rather correct but at the same time eager to please, a man who never missed the chance of doing business. He wore starched collars which shone like porcelain and this porcelain shininess was reflected in his pale, rather fidgety, fresh grey eyes.

'Not quite a thrush-egg blue, as we were saying – '

'I rather think we had a roll of shantung in something of that shade,' Walpole said. 'A customer ordered it and then some friend or other told her the colour was unlucky. I think we might still have it. If we have it'll probably be stowed away somewhere in my office. I'll have to look it out.'

Maisie thanked him and Walpole went on to say:

'Are you going to be at home again this afternoon, Miss Foster? If I find it I could snip a length off and drop it in as I go out to tea. I generally go across to the Geisha for a cup about half past four.'

It was nearly five o'clock before Walpole did in fact arrive and she was then astonished to see that he carried a small box of water colour paints in his hand. The roll of shantung, he explained, was not in his office after all; but in his eagerness to please, always keen to do business, he was ready to mix blues of all sorts until the right one was found.

'It's awfully good of you,' Maisie said. 'I'm afraid if you want water for the paints we'll have to go upstairs. Do you mind?'

Maisie's small sitting-room upstairs, with its window overlooking the churchyard, had all the embalmed silence of a cloister. It was a mild late spring afternoon and a tree of double white cherry had shed a snowstorm of petals on grass, gravestones and path below. Looking down at it Walpole remarked to Maisie on the surprising isolation of it all. He would never have guessed how quiet she was here, how comfortable, how tucked away.

'If we can mix this colour right,' he said, 'I'm going to London tomorrow myself and I'll try to match it up.'

As he sat at a table, mixing and then painting strips of colour on a sheet of white paper, she couldn't help noticing that his hands were of surprising thinness. The fingers were long and exploratory. They were the kind of hands pianists are popularly supposed to have and she half-expected him to start playing tunes with paints and paint-brush.

'I hope you've had tea,' she said. Walpole was being exceptionally studious and careful with his mixing of colours, she thought, and it was already half past five. 'Because if you haven't –'

'I had to cut it, I'm afraid,' he said. 'I got held up by a long telephone call.'

'Oh! I'll get some,' she said. 'I haven't had mine yet.'

He thanked her with his usual eagerness that was also in some contradictory way so correct.

'Would you care for me to bring some sample buttons too if I can get them?' he said over tea.

She said she would, very much, and after that they talked with triviality of the dressmaking trade, how fussy customers sometimes were, what stupid things they said and how absurdly they contradicted themselves. She several times said 'Oh! yes, Oh! don't they?' in delighted and surprised exclamation at some point he made.

'Of course I've seen you often in the shop,' he said, 'but I don't suppose I've ever really spoken to you.'

'No, I suppose not, really.'

'I suppose I'm always at the grindstone. I'm often at the shop by half past six in the morning and sometimes I don't leave till nine or ten at night.'

'Not much time at home. What does Mrs Walpole say to it all?'

'Oh! she reads a lot,' he said. 'I suppose she's sort of conditioned herself to it. After all, in business –'

He seemed, she thought, to speak of his wife with indifference, as of another piece of material rolled up, put away and waiting to be used.

'I think perhaps if we concentrated on these four samples,' he said, 'and I could try to get something in that range –'

Some of the blues were really exquisite, she suddenly told him. They really were. She herself thought he was really very artistic.

'Oh? you think so? I did do some painting at one time. I used to do designs on fabrics, but I gave it up. The business came first.'

'You should never have given it up,' she said. 'You have just the right sort of hands.'

Soon he was packing up the paint-box, ready to go; the business called; in his eager way he was thanking her for the tea.

'It was excellent, the tea. Far better than I get at the Geisha.' He laughed. 'You should start a little tea-place of your own.'

'You're always welcome to a cup,' she said. 'Any day. I usually have mine about four.'

After that he started to discover, almost every day, some sort of excuse to come across the square at four o'clock. Some new buttons had arrived; he had spotted, in a fashion magazine or somewhere, a new design for a collar; he had bought new, delightful silks from Italy.

In the churchyard laburnum blossom succeeded cherry; the summer began to grow hot. Walpole started to wear a light cream linen jacket, but sometimes in the humid mid afternoons he took even this off and sat sipping tea with Maisie in his shirt-sleeves in the stifling little upstairs room.

One afternoon it seemed hotter than ever and she got up to draw the curtains. She didn't like drawing the curtains, she explained to Walpole; it might make people think that some-one had died. Then as she reached up to draw them she turned suddenly and found him standing close to her, lips parted, fresh grey eyes more fidgety, more eager than ever. For some seconds she stood there transfixed in the act of drawing the curtains, one arm uplifted, her dress stretched tight across her breast. A moment later he was kissing her and with two swift sharp snaps she drew the curtains together, shutting out any possible gazer from the churchyard and the light of the hot midsummer afternoon.

The two snaps of the curtains were the first of several signals that started to release the coiled spring inside her. At first the process was neither violent nor abrupt. It was much more like the unfolding of a flower. It didn't even show itself in thrilling outward signs, in coquettishness or laughing responses, in the customary half-articulate light-headed reactions of girls suddenly awakened. Her only visible sign of change was that she started to be a little more meticulous about her hair in the afternoons.

She had in fact suddenly become acutely conscious of her hair and one afternoon, after two or three weeks of meeting Walpole, she brushed it vigorously out and then put it up, in a sort of brown pinnacle, in an entirely different way.

When Walpole later arrived he was quick to notice the change. It made her look so much taller, he said, it seemed to lift her up. He gazed at it for some moments with a sort of compressed rapture and then in a sudden spontaneous gesture took it in both hands, slowly smoothing it upwards.

These long slow movements of his hands on her hair were the next signals in the process of awakening. A crowd of nerves at the roots of her hair, low in the neck, started to quiver like an unrestrained chorus of strings. She found it suddenly impossible to hold still and presently she and Walpole were half sitting, half lying in a chair, embracing violently, he still smoothing her hair upwards, with one hand.

'You know how to drive me mad now, don't you?' became a phrase of hers, repeated over and over again, during the next few hot weeks of summer.

By this time the spring inside her, so long coiled up, had become completely released in all its strength. She now started to shut the front door at five, giving up the meeting for tea at four, so that Walpole could slip in when the last of her customers had departed.

Throughout the hot afternoons of July she continually lay undressed on the bed upstairs, listening to, though over and over again not really hearing, a recital from Walpole on an age-old, long-familiar theme. It was not that his wife was cold, undemonstrative or casually unreceptive of the things he wanted to give – it was merely that he was lonely. He had been lonely for a long, long time. That was why he was often so early at business and away so late at night. That was why, cursed with loneliness, he was so glad of Maisie.

After a time, she discovered, she herself began to be bored with this theme and it was with something like relief that she heard him say, one afternoon towards the end of July:

'I've got bad news. I'm going away for a couple of weeks or so. I've simply got to give her a holiday. We're going down to Bournemouth in the car. By God, I shall miss you.'

'I shall be here when you get back,' she said, calmly and quietly. 'Waiting. Just the same.'

But when he got back, nearly three weeks later, it was not the same.

The interval woke her fully to a disturbing, almost intolerable reality. She now discovered, and with something like despair as time went on, that the one thing she missed more than anything else was Walpole's simple ability to make her excited, almost mad. She wanted above all to feel the smooth, long hands slowly driving her to an exquisite distraction through the roots of her hair.

One of her customers about this time was a robust, middle-aged countrywoman named Miss Walker. She had a habit of wearing men's shirts with green bow ties, heavy tweed skirts, thick brogue shoes and a sort of green Tyrolean hat. She was extremely particular about the shirts. She liked them to be hand-made; she specially insisted also that they should be made from the sort of material obtainable only from men's shops. 'Not from that wretched *Bon Marché* or Walpole's.'

A gentlemen's outfitters named Sampson & Marshall kept the shirting materials on which Miss Walker so meticulously insisted and late one morning she was in there, selecting several lengths for Maisie to make up. As she stood at the counter a young man in a light fawn check suit, neat brown shoes and a light brown trilby hat came in and began to inquire about shirts made to measure.

'I'm afraid we don't do them, sir,' the assistant said. 'There really isn't all that call – '

Miss Walker, overhearing, said in a peremptory way that of course there was a call. Here, in fact, was a call. They were all too conservative and stereotyped in the clothing business, she announced, in the matter of shirts especially. They needed a jolly good jolt from time to time.

'Miss Foster will make them up for you. She's quite first class. She's always made shirts for me. I'm selecting some materials now.'

In her robust, forthright way she went on to tell the young man that she herself was in fact going back to Miss Foster's premises immediately and if he cared to come along –

He thanked her and presently they were walking through the town together. It turned out that he had only just come to the town, was a cashier at a bank and had a temporary room at The George Hotel. No, he confessed to her, he didn't like the town. It was dull, it bored him, especially on Sundays. It drove you mad on Sundays.

'Do you hunt at all?' Miss Walker said.

'I'm afraid not.'

'Pity. I could have introduced you to the hunting crowd.'

Half an hour later she left him alone with Maisie. His name, he told Maisie, was Robert Prentice. When he removed his jacket so that she could measure him for the shirts it became obvious that he was not very well built but quite muscular in a sinewy sort of way. The shoulders were narrow; the waist and hips were fined down. A certain shyness of manner, though not excessive, merely emphasized the physical qualities and the thought crossed her mind that he might possibly have found it difficult to make friends.

Soon he was telling her, as he had told Miss Walker, of his boredom with the town, especially the Sunday boredom. For Heaven's sake what did a man do in a town like this on Sundays? What for example did she do on Sundays?'

'Me?' she said. 'Well now, what do I do on Sundays?'

She had finished taking his measurements and he was already putting on his jacket. 'Well, I get up rather late, about half past ten, I suppose. I don't have any breakfast, just a cup of tea. Then I cook myself a really good meal – I don't have much chance to do that in the week – and sit down about two o'clock to eat it. Generally roast beef and Yorkshire.'

'Sounds wonderful,' he said. He interposed here a brief description of the remarkable roast beef and Yorkshire served on Sundays at The George Hotel. It was in the cat's meat class, he explained, generally tepid and smothered always in a brown congealing paste that passed as gravy. 'But that's only half your day. What about the rest?'

As she went on to tell him that after lunch she invariably read the papers, had tea about five o'clock, and then in the evening had a leisurely hot bath, she looked instinctively at his hands. For a well-built man they were unexpectedly small hands, far shorter than Walpole's. She was greatly surprised about this; and instinctively too, as she looked at them, she seemed already to feel them stroking the roots of her hair.

If her surprise about his hands was great his own about Maisie was far greater. He had expected a much older woman. She was in fact of his own age and presently he found himself saying:

'But don't you ever go out on Sundays?'

'Never,' she said. 'Where is there to go? The cinemas don't open. I hardly ever drink. And you'd hardly expect me to eat lunch at The George, would you? No, I like it here.'

All this time her eyes were insidiously and consistently drawn back to his hands. For this reason she hardly ever looked him fully in the face, with the result that he somehow gained the impression that she too, with her colourless, unprepossessing appearance, was shy.

Presently he was saying:

'I hope you didn't mind my asking all that just now, but I just wondered – '

'Wondered what?'

'I wondered if you'd perhaps like to come out with me on Sunday?'

Again she stood watching his hands; again she seemed to feel the touch of them on the nape of her neck.

'Where would we go?' she said. 'What would we do? What could we do if it rained?'

He hardly knew, he said. Of course the situation would have been easy if he had had a car, but unfortunately a bank clerk's salary didn't run to that. As he said this he threw up his hands rather demonstratively, in a gesture of resignation that bemused her completely. A sudden unbearable web of tension spun itself round her, trapping her as if she were a fly.

'It's very nice of you to ask me,' she said and the words came thickly, almost congealed, in her throat, 'but I tell you what –'

'Yes?'

'If it wouldn't bore you too much you could come and share Sunday lunch with me here.'

He reacted with almost pitiful delight. It was the nicest thing that had happened to him since he came to the town. She couldn't imagine how much he'd look forward to it. She couldn't have asked him a nicer thing.

He arrived soon after one o'clock the following Sunday, a thunderously warm day already humidly overcast but as yet without rain, carrying as gifts for her a box of burnt almond chocolates and a bottle of *Johannisberger Riesling* – perhaps not the best thing to drink with roast beef, he confessed, but the best The George could do.

'It's really more than kind of you,' she said. 'I hardly ever have wine.'

All through lunch thunder hammered at the distances. The smell of roast beef, made richer by the oppressive quality of the air and then by the cool white wine, drifted almost voluptuously about the little upper room.

Several times during the course of the meal Maisie confessed that she was afraid of thunder. She was really a coward about thunder. Among other things she had a dreadful premonition that one day the church would be struck and the spire come tumbling down. He was inclined to laugh at all this and when he laughed it was not merely in the gay fashion of a man completely happy but also as if released from something, set free at last from his Sabbath bondage.

Somewhere about three o'clock a single snarl of thunder seemed actually, as she had always dreaded, to bounce off the church spire. Within a second she was shouting to him to draw the curtains. He leapt up and drew them quickly, plunging the little room into almost total darkness while the rain, beginning at last, teemed torrentially outside.

For a few seconds he found himself actually having to grope his way back to his chair. He asked her if she was all right, if it was true she was really afraid, and in passing her chair put his hands, more by accident than anything, on her shoulders. They were trembling. In an instant her hands sprang up and grasped his own and pressed the fingers against her hair.

She spent the rest of the afternoon in his arms, in a luxurious and tempestuous trance heightened by her genuine fear of the storm. It seemed as if the rain would never stop. The air became yellow with the strangest of thunder lights. Whenever the clock on the church chimed it was on cavernous notes, echo repeating echo, uncannily oppressive and near.

It was six o'clock before the rain stopped and she could draw back the curtains. She was calmer now. The storm sailed suddenly and completely away, taking her fears with it as surely as a kite dragging its tail. The effect of the wine, which had at first made her sleepy, had worn off by this time and now she was herself again.

'I've loved it here,' he said, 'absolutely loved it. When am I going to see you again?'

'Next Sunday?'

'Not before? I hoped – '

'I don't think so. I really have so little time in the week.' She was thinking already, not precisely in a calculating sort of way, but quite coolly, that Walpole would be back by Tuesday.

'You see I'm busy all day. Then I have to get a meal and there are always accounts to do.'

Choked with disappointment, he could only murmur, as Walpole had so often done, that it was all so lonely in the week, so damned lonely. Once again the words bored her and she said:

'You mustn't let yourself be lonely. I'm alone here but not lonely. Think of me. I shall think of you.'

'You will?'

'Of course. A lot. Yes, you can see me next Sunday. You can come to lunch again.'

'Thank you. That's wonderful.'

'Don't you really think it's perhaps a good thing if we don't see each other for a week?' she said. 'After all you hardly know me.'

'I could get to know you more if I saw you in the week.'

A renewed desire to be caressed again suddenly overcame her and she put her head on his shoulder, at the same time raising one of his hands to her hair.

'You'll have heaps of time to get to know me next Sunday,' she said. 'Sunday's always a long day.'

The following week Walpole came back with distractions of his own. As if three weeks of hotel life were not enough, his wife had developed moods. With petulance she refused breakfasts, didn't get up until midday and left him to walk by the sea alone. In the enervating southern air he drowsed away long empty days under pines, building up a brittle edifice of self-pity, telling himself that he was lonelier than ever and longing above all for a glimpse of Maisie, so unexpectedly superb in body, in the little upper room.

As if nothing had happened in his absence she took him back into the quietness of her special seclusion as she might have picked up a dress that had been laid aside unfinished. She slipped off her clothes for him with no more compunction than if she had been taking off a hat and with hardly a thought of Robert Prentice. It was wonderful to be caressed again. It was

wonderful to feel also that when both the week's ecstasy and
boredom had built themselves up to be equally intolerable
there would be a change of hands on Sunday.

'Did you miss me?' Walpole said. 'Did anything happen
while I was away?'

Of course she missed him. But nothing had happened at all.

It never once occurred to her that there might have been some
sort of deceit in this. If anybody were being deceitful it was
Walpole. What she did with Robert Prentice actually took
place, as it seemed to her, in a world apart, a privileged, private
world in which Walpole had no place.

'I've got a surprise for you,' Walpole said and asked her to
shut her eyes.

When she opened them again it was to find herself holding
a necklace of amethysts, particularly dark ones of burning
violet, set in gold.

'Oh! I've never had jewellery. Never really before. I
couldn't afford it. I always said I'd never have any if I couldn't
afford the best.'

Later that afternoon Walpole found himself in stunned
contemplation of the most extraordinary vision he had ever
seen in his life: that of Maisie lying full-length on the bed,
wearing nothing but the amethysts. This one glowing piece of
decoration had the effect of even making her unprepossessing
face, with its colourless, tepid skin, seem celestially ravishing,
so that he actually went down on his knees to her, hopelessly,
almost prayerfully entranced.

The effect on him of incidents of this kind, however, did
more than merely entrance him. He began to speak of divorce.
He announced that he would go to his wife, tell everything and
beg for release from her. He would marry Maisie, bejewel
her, make her a partner in the business, set her up on a plane of
such delight that she would realize, he assured her, that life had
really only just begun.

Maisie was silently horrified. She shrank from divorce and
all its distasteful associations as from something leprous. She

wanted no part of the complications of courts, lawyers or, even business. To be caressed, in isolation, was enough. It gave her refined excitements; it left her free of obligations.

'You must think carefully before you take a step like that,' she said to Walpole. 'It's something you might regret for ever.'

'Are you trying to say that you wouldn't marry me if I got the divorce?'

'I'm saying it's something I'd have to think about.'

'You mean you don't love me?'

'I've never said I loved you. I like being with you. I like all the things we do together. Otherwise I wouldn't do them. But love – I don't know about that.'

Her apparent calmness in the face of a situation Walpole regarded as both complex and critical made his own confusions infinitely worse. Beyond confusion he could see, he thought, new and impossible wastes of loneliness; beyond loneliness only intolerable despair.

He started not to be able to sleep at nights; he wandered about the house, playing interminable games of patience, drinking whisky until the small hours. At business he presented the crumpled appearance of a blind that had been badly rolled up and as badly unrolled again. Creased and slack, he groped at the simplest of problems and accepted defeat with the limpness of a man half-sick. In the eventual and necessary act of pulling himself together he went about barking, hostile as an ill-tempered dog.

When he begged Maisie to let him come to see her more often and even suggested Sunday as a new field in which they could be alone together he took her refusal as meaning another withdrawal of affection. Compassionately she begged him not to be silly, to take life easy, to live for the day; but in renewed moods of self-pity he could only feel that salt was being rubbed into the open sores of his soul.

'But why not Sunday? It would be simple. All day together.'

'Because Sunday is my day. I share it with myself.'

The fact that she always shared most of it with Robert Prentice never struck her as being a fresh deceit or as being a source of danger, perhaps even a source of complexities so potentially twisted that they might perhaps grow tragic. She was free; she could please herself who she spent her days and nights with. As quiet as ever, she even drew satisfaction from lying awake at night, imagining first that Walpole was making love to her, then that Prentice was the one beside her in the bed. It was nice to compare their idiosyncrasies, their differing ways of expressing affection: Walpole cooler, slower, older, but skilled in the final, passionate act of satisfaction; Prentice spirited and quick, warm and excited even to the extent, sometimes, of being lyrical.

Robert Prentice begged too to see her more often. Couldn't he come in during the evenings sometimes? He finished pretty early these days at the bank; the evenings were awfully long and deadly.

Her answer was almost word for word the one she always gave to Walpole:

'The evenings are my own. I share them with myself. After all I have a long hard day.'

He too took it to mean, as he felt it only could mean, a rejection of love. He too started brooding. There was an actual ache in his heart, stone-like, as he went on long walks, wretchedly beating out the oppressive minutes till Sunday. She in turn begged him, as she had begged Walpole, to take their friendship as nothing more than friendship, to enjoy her company like a glass of wine.

'Let's just get a little intoxicated, then sleep it off and start all over again.'

It was impossible for his brooding soul to make sense of advice of that kind and one Sunday it seemed to her that, if driven much farther into himself, he might actually start weeping. She tried to counteract this boring possibility by making him drink another glass or two of wine and then, when that didn't work, had a better idea.

She excused herself, saying she wanted to powder her nose, and went into her bedroom. After five minutes she called him, saying she had something to show him, a surprise, and would he come in?

A few moments later he was staring down at the same vision that had so shatteringly distracted Walpole: that of Maisie lying full-length on the bed, naked except for Walpole's necklace of glowing purple fire.

As he saw her he did not bow down, as Walpole had done, with prayerful entrancement. He simply laughed with an amazed joy. 'I thought that might cheer you up,' she said and she laughed too. It seemed a nice sort of joke to her.

And then, two or three weeks later, something else of unexpected importance happened. She met a third and far more interesting man.

Breezily and busily he stepped into her life on a warm morning in late September: a traveller in electric sewing machines named Archie Bishop.

'You want the best sewing machines? I got 'em. You want service? I give. You want to pay by instalment? I got the longest instalment plan since Delilah cut off Sampson's hair.'

Quick as an eel, Archie Bishop never allowed his body a single breath in which to be still. His hands were semaphoric flags, flashing messages everywhere. His small brown eyes popped about in the volatile fashion of knobs of pop-corn dancing up and down in a patent street-corner cooker. His neat golden moustache sparked with points of gingery fire.

'Now, Miss Foster, we have three models. There's the Olympus, the new de-luxe. Then there's the Diana – bigger and better than Dors. And the Sheraton – the super-duper, out-and-outer. It does everything but make the tea.'

'But I – '

'You'll do twice as much work in half the time and have bags of time left for having fun you never thought you could afford even if you'd got the time which you never had. Now where could I do a demonstration?'

'Listen,' Maisie said. 'I do not want an electric sewing machine.'

'You mean you think you don't want one.' A spontaneous, friendly laugh, about the twentieth of the morning, split the air. 'There's nothing so think but meaning makes it so.'

'Also, if you don't mind,' Maisie said, 'I don't happen to have electricity.'

'We'll put it in!' Archie Bishop said. 'I'll halve my commission and pay for it myself!' He permitted himself the luxury of an abrupt, stunned laugh. 'You haven't what? Madam, in this day and age! *You have not got electricity?* Shades of Benjamin Franklin. I grow faint, Miss Foster. I fail – '

'I manage perfectly well with gas,' Maisie said. 'It suits me perfectly – '

'So you're cooking with gas, now?' he said, in mock American accents. 'Great. Why not charcoal burners?'

'Look, I'm awfully sorry, but I'm very, very busy – '

'Busy? We're all busy. Those who aren't busy are dead.' His hands made sharp concessionary contortions in the air. 'Very well. As you wish. My time is yours. I can come back whenever you say. After lunch. After tea. Tomorrow. Next week. Christmas Eve, Good Friday – '

'I'm sorry, I don't want the machine. I don't want a demonstration. I don't want anything. Besides, it's lunch time.'

'Have lunch with me!'

'No thanks. I close for the lunch hour. I have to get my own.'

'I can cook. I make omelettes. They look like leather. Chamois leather.' Another laugh, infectious this time, actually caused Maisie to forget herself and break into a brief spontaneous giggle. He was quick to seize on this unexpected gesture of friendliness and said: 'I must say I like the dress. I like the little itsy-bitsy, forget-me-notty, little-bit-of-spotty, polka-dot – '

Maisie was wearing a neat sleeveless dress of white linen

covered in pale blue polka dots. The day was warm for late September, but in the dress she looked quiet, composed, and cool.

'Make it yourself?'

'I did.'

'You don't need an electric sewing machine, Miss Foster,' he said with sudden mock seriousness. 'You have an angelic needle, dear lady. Quite an angelic needle. Bishop, you clueless moron, what in the name of holy silkworms are you up to?'

'For goodness' sake, go and have your lunch,' Maisie said. 'Do.'

'Splendid thought! But I'll be back.' He laughed, took out a diary stuffed with dates, notes, addresses, and figures, flipped over its leaves and said: 'Now let's see. I've got two aged widows to rob at half past two. A blind spinster at three o'clock and – how about five o'clock?'

Five o'clock, Walpole's hour, was utterly out of the question and for a second Maisie broke out of her customary quietness with a real bark of vexation:

'Now for goodness' sake get out, will you? I've had all I can stand. You're enough to drive a saint up the wall. For the last time I am very very busy. I've got an order for a wedding to finish and I'll probably be working till midnight –'

'Ravishing thought.'

'Please. Do you mind?'

'Sorry, sorry, sorry, sorry.'

Suddenly, without argument or another quip or protest, Archie Bishop was gone.

Maisie immediately locked her door, went upstairs, and set about boiling herself an egg and making a cup of tea for lunch. Then suddenly she began to feel ashamed of herself for having lost her temper. She felt rather as if she had unjustly scolded a small boy for having played a practical joke on her.

She ate her lunch moodily. She felt she would have given a good deal to retract the words hurled in temper at Archie

Bishop. It was all very small and undignified and as the afternoon went on the incident started to haunt her.

'Oh! well he deserved it. It *was* enough to make you boil. It's nothing to fuss about now. People like that get what they deserve.'

But when Walpole dropped in, as always, about five o'clock, she was still moody, still distracted by self-reproaches.

'No, you really can't come upstairs today. I haven't even time to stop for tea.'

'But why?'

'There simply isn't the time, that's why. I've got this wedding order to finish and it has to be done. It has to be right.'

'You seem short-tempered today.'

'Perhaps I am.'

'Is it my fault?'

'I never said it was, but if you like to think so, if you like to think so.'

The immediate effect of the incident was to drive Walpole further into himself. He withdrew into darker realms of self-pity. He started a parade of anguished suspicions about her. There was another man; he was sure of it; she had another lover.

The effect on her was precisely the opposite. She felt increasingly self-critical. She worked on the wedding order restlessly, her mind continually snapping at itself. She even began to feel rebellious, for the first time in her life, against seclusion. She wanted to drop everything, rush out and get away somewhere.

As evening came on she locked the front door and went on working, striving hard to get the wedding order done. About seven o'clock rain started to fall, bringing down the first big papery chestnut leaves in the churchyard. The sound of rain and leaves, in some way ghostly, did nothing to subdue her restlessness and presently she found herself listening for another sound, that of a knock on the door, of Archie Bishop coming back.

She finished the wedding order about half past eleven, then made herself some coffee and took it to bed with her.

'I make omelettes. They look like leather. Chamois leather. I've got two aged widows to rob at half past two. You have an angelic needle, dear lady. An angelic needle. What in the name of holy silkworms? There's nothing so think but meaning makes it so.'

She lay awake for a long time, not thinking so much as working a treadmill of words. Stupid, gay, bright idiotic phrases sounded in prancing dances, never letting her rest. Little forces, inspired by little gestures, looks and bursts of laughter, marched in on her throughout the night.

Six months before she would have laughed at herself at the notion of having electricity installed simply because a stranger had slightly mocked her about it; but within a week of that slightly crazy and inconclusive morning meeting with Archie Bishop workmen were in the house, fitting the cables.

In the installation of electricity she found another excuse to put first Walpole and then Robert Prentice a little farther away from her.

'The house is an absolute pigsty. No, you really can't come in. There isn't anywhere to sit down even. The bedroom is piled with clutter and you can't turn round. And you know how workmen are – they'll be ages and ages.'

The two men, pushed out, brooded in their separate backwaters. The vision of Maisie on the bed, amethyst-clothed, persisted for each of them like a nightmare.

In turn she had almost succeeded in putting Archie Bishop out of her mind when suddenly, on a morning in October fresh with a touch of frost, she heard a muted whistle at the front door and a voice saying:

'Digging for buried treasure? Ducats or diamonds? Wouldn't Benjamin be pleased?'

Archie Bishop, in a new herring-bone pattern overcoat of smart light grey, came breezily into Maisie's workshop as if life had spurned him in no single instant or particular since she had seen him last. He seemed, if anything, smarter, brighter, more inconsequential than ever.

'More wedding orders today?'

'Not today.'

'Ah! then possibly we might have the little tête-à-tête?'

'I still don't want the electric sewing machine if that's what you're trying to say.'

The first engaging, effervescent laugh of the morning bubbled about the air.

'I no longer sell electric sewing machines, dear lady. It proved to be *très, très difficile*. It came to pass that I actually found some people who hadn't got electricity. Not playing the game. Very awkward.'

Her normally pallid face suddenly flushed darkly. Neither Walpole nor Robert Prentice had ever said a single word, in sarcasm or fun, to hurt her; in devotion both were blameless. But suddenly the mischief in Archie Bishop's words went through her like a twisting needle. There were almost tears in her eyes.

'No. Refrigerators now. Every man's ice-box. Own your own igloo. Ever go to the flicks? Saw a film about Eskimoes the other day. Simple chaps. I believe you could sell them a refrigerator at that.'

'*You* could.' Her voice, if not quite bitter, carried sarcastic undertones that were not lost on him. 'You could sell anybody anything.'

'Now that,' Archie Bishop said, again with the friendliest of laughs, 'is what is known as coming the old acid.'

'Whatever that may mean.'

'You know what I always say – there's nothing so mean but thinking makes it so.'

'I thought,' she said, 'it was the other way round?'

'Revised version,' he said in the briskest of voices. 'Winter season. All jokes now kept in the deep freeze. Now what about the fridge? Not until you've had one will you realize what pineapple and ice can do when you put them into a marriage bed of cream –'

Whereas, a moment or two before, she had been on the verge of tears she now found herself giving another rather foolish, spontaneous giggle.

'I suppose you talk to everyone like this?' she said. 'Even the aged widows?'

'Given up robbing aged widows,' he said. 'I concentrate solely on young ones now. And married women.'

'How nice,' she said. 'That lets me out.'

'The loss is mine.'

'And what will you do,' Maisie said, 'when you can't sell any more refrigerators?'

'I propose,' he said, 'to sell concrete mixers to Socialist conferences.'

'Yes?' she said. 'How will that help?'

'Oh! very much,' he said. 'Everyone will be able to mix his own concrete conclusions. In seven separate flavours.'

She laughed again. A sudden strange light-heartedness, of a kind she had never experienced before, ripped quickly through her, leaving her feeling inconsequential too. She had never in her life heard anyone talk as Archie Bishop talked. Every quip, each piece of nonsense thrown off as a conjurer throws off an act, found her unready.

Upstairs a workman started hammering and outside, across the churchyard, the clock chimed half past twelve. The two events made Archie Bishop lift his head smartly, rather like a handsome cockerel, and say that it was time for a snifter and wouldn't Maisie nip out and join him in one somewhere?

'Oh! I don't drink much, thank you. And certainly not in the middle of a working day. Goodness, I'd go to sleep all afternoon.'

And what, Archie Bishop wanted to know, was wrong with that?

'Nothing, I suppose. Only –'

'Only what? Me? – I always sleep all afternoon. Often.

Have half a dozen drinks and a good lunch and then go and lie down in a hayfield somewhere.'

'You're not serious. Don't you have to work?'

'Work? What's work? The man who invented it should have been choked with his dummy tit. Come on, let's go and have one.'

All that had happened to her in life, everything of excitement or importance, had hitherto happened in seclusion. In the isolation of the little house she had discovered, by the purest chance, what revolution a simple caress from Walpole could begin; it had been fun to repeat it with Prentice. Now it was exactly as if Archie Bishop had opened a door; at any moment, she felt, the façade of seclusion would start crumbling and melting away.

'Come on, I'll give you lunch. We'll have a couple of snifters and then lunch. And then we'll take a boat out on the river for the afternoon.'

'I never heard of anything so absurd.'

'No? Just shows you haven't known Archie from Karachi very long.' He mocked her gaily, now in the accents of an Eastern gentleman. 'I sell you big fine carpet? – '

'You came to sell me a fridge and here we are boating – '

'Oh! blow the fridge.'

'I was going to say I'd probably buy one.'

'Haven't the heart to take the money, lady. Well, not today, anyway. By the way, what's your other name?'

'Maisie.'

'Maisie, Maisie, give me your answer, do. Will you have lunch with me and boat at half past two?'

'No, thank you,' she said. 'My lunch is all prepared and I've got to work this afternoon.'

Soon he again breezed light-heartedly away, leaving her to her solitary lunch upstairs. Since the electricians were still busy in the sitting-room she ate her meal of cold ham and salad in the bedroom. Across the churchyard the October afternoon glowed like a golden fruit; in the square the chestnuts burned richly in the sun. She had never before felt lonely in isolation; now she began to feel inexplicably, uncannily restless. She felt herself struggling against seclusion as a chrysalis struggles to free itself after winter.

At three o'clock Archie Bishop breezed back again, refreshed with four double gins, a lunch of chicken pie and chocolate ice-cream and two cold beers. By no means drunk, he surveyed her on the contrary with an air almost sober, apologetically.

'Played the fool a bit this morning. Of course I've got to work. As a matter of fact I've got to go over to see a man at Abingford. Wondered if you'd care to come for the drive? Serious, this time. Glorious afternoon.'

All afternoon she had dreaded the arrival of Walpole; with something like dismay she had looked forward to the five o'clock visit, the fretting frustrations, the soul-searchings.

'I'd love to come,' she said.

He drove his car slowly. The sky was like a thin azure globe. Empty wheatfields caught the clear sunlight and lay like silky yellow squares against greenest patterns of meadowland. In the immense embalming peace of October the colouring trees hardly stirred.

After four or five miles he stopped the car at the crest of the river valley. Down below, the river wound clear blue through wide meadows where red and white cattle grazed not unlike crowds of quiet ladybirds.

'Peaceful,' he said. 'Could sleep.'

'Me too.'

For ten minutes or more he slept quite soundlessly. At first she shut her eyes too, but soon she felt restless and opened them. The chrysalis was stirring again and she sat staring in contemplation first at the valley below and then at Archie Bishop, no longer the clowning cockerel of the morning but a man sunk into an amazing trance of tranquillity.

When he opened his eyes it was to find her still staring into his face.

'That's a nice sight to wake up to,' he said and turned slowly, kissing her fully and quickly on the mouth.

'Just for luck,' he said, with the merest touch of former lightness. 'A free gift.'

'Why luck?'

'Everybody needs a little now and then.'

'You treat all the girls like this? Don't tell me you don't, because you do.'

'Those who know should never ask,' he said. 'Yes: absolutely right. Come one, come all. Married or single. Young or old. Same treatment.'

'It's comforting for all of us to know where we stand.'

'Of course. I'm a fair-minded man.'

'Do you suppose,' she said, 'there'll ever be one who'll be luckier than the rest?'

' "I doubt it," said the carpenter, and shed a bitter tear.'

He grinned and then soberly, and for a little longer this time, kissed her a second time. To her astonishment the kiss had on her much the same effect as the embalming October afternoon. It seemed to seal all her emotions somewhere down in the deep core of herself, filling her with a profound and unexpected satisfaction.

She felt, in her amazement, that she had to say something about this, and after staring down for some time at the meadows she said:

'It was a big surprise, kissing you. I didn't think it would be like that with you.'

'Ah. The lady tactfully expresses disappointment.'

'No,' she said. 'I just didn't think it would be like that, that's all.'

'Not quite enough zip?' he said. She could feel the quips feeding themselves into his mouth, like bullets into a gun. 'Of course I have other techniques.'

Quietly she turned and took his face into her two hands, holding it there for fully half a minute before speaking.

'It was very moving,' she said.

That evening, alone, she sat down and wrote two letters, in reality the same letter: one to Walpole and the other to Robert Prentice.

'It must have been obvious to you for some time that this couldn't go on. It isn't that I'm not fond of you. It isn't that at all. It's simply that the longer we go on the worse the complications will be. It simply wouldn't be fair to you if I let you go on thinking that I loved you or that I might perhaps love you in time. I know now that I never have – please will you try very hard to forgive me this? – and that I'm sure I never will.'

After she had been out to post the letters she went back to her room and sat for some time looking out of her window at the clear night sky. An autumnal planet of great splendour, setting with a ripe glow in the west, seemed to reflect in the calmest distillation all the peace of the golden afternoon.

As she sat there she started to think of Archie Bishop: not so much of the clowning cockerel with the facile quips, the carelessness and the quick magical banter, as of the few serious moments in the car, apparently on the surface light-hearted too, when she had finally confessed to him:

'I'll count all the minutes till you come back. I will, really. Don't be more than a week if you can help it, please. Promise me?'

With the lightest of promises Archie Bishop declared his earnest intention of being back in no time at all. The bad penny, he reminded her, the bad penny.

Again, and for almost a minute, she held his face in her hands. The chrysalis was moving now in its final tortuous struggles to be free and as she kissed him again she was so oblivious of everything outside her that she didn't even bother to lift his hands to her hair. That easy, simple, electrifying gesture was necessary no longer.

'I've never been kissed like that before,' she said. 'I never knew it was such a serious thing.'

Neither Walpole nor Robert Prentice showed even a little willingness to forgive.

After three tortured and intolerable days Robert Prentice borrowed a ·22 shot-gun from the landlord of The George Hotel and, on the pretext of wanting to shoot rabbits, walked down to the river one evening and blew out his brains on the small jetty where townspeople hired boats and punts and did a little sailing at week-ends.

With demented forethought he left a letter for the manager of his bank, expressing sorrow for all he had done, and another to the coroner. In his note to the bank manager, a brief one, he wrote: 'It can't be possible that God had to send me to this town just to meet a woman like Maisie Foster. It just can't be possible. There must be some other sort of mercy I might have been granted.'

With some indiscretion the bank manager, greatly upset, showed the letter to his wife who, under promise of silence, instantly spoke of it to her sister.

When rumour started to poison the town Ashley Walpole went about in solitary horror, trying to nurse a mind broken to near craziness by hideous jealousies. He savagely conceived that he knew, now, why Maisie had written to him, why the turquoise afternoons were now all over. But if he bitterly hated the young man who had been stupid and unstable enough to make an unholy mess of himself at the boating jetty it was no more than mere petulance compared with the thoughts, revengeful to a point of black ghoulishness, that began to obsess him about Maisie. It was now not merely a question of not being able to sleep at nights. He tramped endlessly about the town, carrying an ancient umbrella that he had hastily snatched up either as if for a source of comfort or as a weapon. With this he made wild stupefied threats at the night sky and sometimes the umbrella came violently undone, flapping like a terrified mad bat with broken wings.

Presently the local station sergeant thought it prudent to warn patrolling night constables of the possibility of running

into that raving lunatic, Ashley Walpole, 'who gets savage with
the moon. They say he drinks them dry at the Liberal Club
every night. He hit a steward with an umbrella the other
evening and had to be carted out.'

In final frenzy, late one night towards the end of November,
Walpole half-ran, half-rolled to Maisie's door and struck it
several blows with the handle of the umbrella, a panting
constable following him on heavy steps half a street away.

Maisie, who had not been able to sleep well for some weeks
either, was lying in a trance of recollection about Archie
Bishop when the knocks came. She had waited a long time for
Bishop. With an actual ache in her heart, much as Walpole had
done, she had brooded alone and for a long time on small
things. The little forces made up of looks, gestures, quips and
finally a few revelatory sober kisses had become magnified
until they too were like great dark bats, haunting her.

She came out of the trance in a state of great excitement,
telling herself that only that joker Archie could be knocking
on her door in that way and so late.

She hastily slipped into a dressing-gown and rushed downstairs, only to open the door to a raging frenzy from Walpole,
who started to batter her savagely about the face with the big
bat-like umbrella, shouting:

'I'll kill you. I'll murder you. I'll kill you so help me – '

The threat of murder is a serious matter, more especially
when made within the hearing of a policeman, and at Walpole's
trial the judge was at great pains to point out to the jury that the
court was a court of law, not of morals. Whether or not a
woman had been the lover of one man or even two was irrele-
vant; it was a shocking and wicked thing for her to be confronted, at the door of her own house, in the dead of night,
totally unprepared and defenceless, by a visitor whose palpable
intention it was to kill. A woman had a perfect right to choose or
reject her friends, or even her lovers, as and when she wished,
and however painful such rejection might be to the rejected it
could never in any circumstances be an excuse for taking the

law into his own hands. It was fortunate indeed that a police officer had been in earshot that night, otherwise they might have now been listening to a graver charge. It was fortunate also that the prisoner had previously been a man of excellent, in fact exemplary character, otherwise the sentence might have been far longer than the two years he now imposed.

A shattered Walpole, in stricken silence, listened without hearing a word. He stared into spaces beyond the courtroom with a peculiar, penetrative concentration, eyes half closed, as if searching for a tiny and barely perceptible object in the far distances: a scrap of colour, a turquoise button or even perhaps an amethyst.

As the winter dusks began to close in earlier and earlier Maisie fell once again into her old habit of isolation. She kept herself to herself; she was busy with her needle; she hardly went out at all. She waited quietly, steadfastly, even with a sort of patience, for Archie Bishop, for ever listening to the echo of voices.

'There's nothing so think but meaning makes it so,' was one of the many silly inconsequential phrases that all through the long winter roamed hauntingly about her mind, together with another. 'You have an angelic needle, dear lady. Quite an angelic needle.'

And still a third, putting its constant nagging question into the quietness of the little house: 'Do you suppose there'll ever be one luckier than the rest?' and its great dark bat of an answer:

' "I doubt it," said the carpenter, and shed a bitter tear.'

# The Golden Oriole

Every evening when he came home from the office Mr Mansfield knew that his wife would be hiding from him somewhere. She had been hiding for many years.

It was not always easy, even in a rather large Edwardian house surrounded by dense old shrubberies of laurustinus and lilac and rose and rhododendron, together with a kitchen garden full of apple and pear trees and currant bushes, to find a new place in which to hide away every evening and he tried always to be fair. Even when he guessed where Mrs Mansfield would be hiding – in the early days of their marriage a favourite place in the summer was among the currant bushes and in winter she often buried herself behind the coats and hats hanging in the cloakroom or behind the thick red curtains in the hall – he tried not to guess too soon. It was nice to prolong the sensation of having lost her and then to enjoy, with a sudden skipping thrill, the experience of finding her again, as if for the first time.

Mr Mansfield, who was in insurance, was rather a heavy man of fifty with plummy grey cheeks and slow slate-coloured eyes. His clothes sat on him baggily. Skipping of any kind seemed to be utterly foreign to his nature. He moved gracelessly and when sometimes he was late for the train in the morning he trotted rather than ran the last few yards to the station, feet barely rising from the ground, his floppy trousers giving him an earnest, obedient, elephantine air.

By contrast his wife, though in her middle forties, seemed to have an almost girlish look about her. This seemed largely due to her excessively light fair hair, light in texture as well as tone, in which there was not the faintest trace of grey. Her eyes, a very smooth pale blue, were as fresh as birds' eggs, with the same air of pristine innocence, lightly touched with wonder.

As the years went past she began to find more subtle hiding-places. Sometimes these were so difficult that she eventually had to make small noises, bird-like or mouse-like or even like the purring of a cat, before Mr Mansfield's attention could be finally attracted. She hid on one occasion in a big old-fashioned wheelbarrow, with a piece of dirty sacking over her, so that she might have been mistaken for a sack of potatoes. On another she crept under a large empty barrel, generally used for blanching rhubarb. The open bung-hole of the barrel made it possible for her to spy on Mr Mansfield as he roamed with elephantine caution and concern about the kitchen garden, softly calling 'Prinny! Prinny!' his pet name for her, a diminutive of princess.

'You really are my princess,' he had said to her many years before. 'I want to put you on a throne. I want to keep you there.'

Whenever she was eventually found – she remained undiscovered in the barrel for nearly half an hour – she always broke into a strange splintered sort of laughter. A feeling of fear and joy ran through her and the laughter had a girlish, virginal, half-frightened tone.

'Prinny, my Prinny, I really thought I'd lost you that time.'

One evening in early June Mr Mansfield was padding heavily up the gravel drive towards the house when he suddenly noticed, under the branches of a crimson rhododendron, a dying thrush. He stooped and, with great concern, picked up the bird with both hands, cradling the still warm, white-gold breast in his palms.

'I'll take you into the house,' he said in a crooning sort of voice. 'Milk – warm milk – that's what I'll give you,' and it was almost as if he were speaking to Prinny.

In fact, for once, he had completely forgotten Prinny. In his deep concern for the thrush – he began to give it little sips of milk with the aid of a salt spoon – all thought of Prinny had strangely slipped his mind. It was more than an hour before he thought again of Prinny, his princess, and Prinny's hiding-places.

Meanwhile, in the kitchen, he wrapped the thrush in a piece of flannel and laid it on top of the warm stove. The bird opened its mouth peakily from time to time and glassily rolled an eye. Continuously Mr Mansfield stroked its feathers and murmured words of comfort:

'You'll sing again. Take it quietly. You're going to be all right. I'll see you sing again.'

When at last the bird twitched a wing strongly enough to lift the edge of the flannel Mr Mansfield gave a positive crow of relieved delight. He felt that he wanted to seize the bird and toss it, like a released dove of peace, into the air. His feelings at the slow restoration of life were expressed in that same skipping thrill he always experienced on finding Prinny in her hiding-place.

A moment or two later Prinny walked into the kitchen. Her customary air of innocence, touched with wonder, seemed strained. Her face, unusually pale, seemed almost embalmed behind a stiff transparent shell.

'Wherever have you been? What *are* you doing? Whatever has happened?'

'Happened?' Mr Mansfield said. 'It's the thrush. It was dying – '

'Thrush? But where have you been?'

'Here,' Mr Mansfield said. 'Here. All the time. I've been nursing the thrush. It was in the garden, dying, and I've got it back to life again. It flapped its wing just now – '

Prinny did not appear to be listening. It was on the tip of her tongue to ask Mr Mansfield why he had forgotten to come to find her, but before she could open her mouth the words rolled themselves suddenly into a stony ball. A moment later it seemed to drop with a bruising thud into the deep cavity of her heart and lie there frozen.

At the same time she was aware of another sensation. She

felt a curious hot confusion about her eyes. Mr Mansfield, picking up the thrush and unfolding it with all the considerate tenderness in the world from its swaddling flannel, like a baby, suddenly seemed to her, for the first time in her life, a figure of monstrous irritation.

'Oh! why all the panic about a thrush?' she said and the words, piercingly uttered, were so unlike her that Mr Mansfield actually picked one out and shot at it with an arrow of amazed concern.

'Panic? Panic? Whatever do you mean?'

'I don't know! I don't know!' she said and a moment later ran from the room. 'How should I know?'

They ate supper coldly, hardly speaking. Her jealous brooding on the thrush kept her separate, invested with a sense of ridicule. That evening she had chosen to hide herself in an old aviary, no longer used, at the bottom of the garden, and for an hour or more she had stayed there in isolation, uttering beseeching musical cries, hoping Mr Mansfield would hear her as a bird.

'It was merely that I couldn't bear to see it dying,' Mr Mansfield told her several times. 'I *was* coming to find you – of course I was – '

She had no answer to give. The joy of hiding and being found seemed, for once, a stupid thing.

For a few evenings she made no hiding-place for herself. She sat instead on the lawn, in a deck-chair, in open view, reading or sewing or merely staring at the flowers.

'Ah! there you are,' Mr Mansfield said, with an enforced cordiality that might have been born of surprise, as if in fact she had been hiding and he had really found her. 'Train was a bit late, I'm afraid.'

Mr Mansfield's kiss on her forehead brought no response from her. She merely looked about her coldly.

Then, after a few evenings, she relented. It was childish to sulk, she told herself. It was silly to be stubborn. It was unthinkable that she should never again hide away and, having hidden, taste the joy of being found.

She decided at last to hide in an apple tree. That particular June evening was exceptionally warm and sultry; on the house wall, facing south, a thousand yellow roses were in bloom, big soft curds of petals spreading fragrance even as far as the apple tree, where she sat half-curled up in the mass of leaves.

For some time she waited with excitement, listening. The train, she told herself several times, was late again. Then, looking at her watch, she made the astonishing discovery that in her excitement she had entirely mistaken the time. She had really hidden herself a full hour too soon.

In the brooding sultry afternoon she dropped into a doze. Presently she vaguely heard what she thought was the sound of a thrush battering a snail on a path and she woke with the beginnings of a renewed irritation that vanished when she realized that the sound was really that of footsteps coming up the drive. Mr Mansfield was home.

Then she heard the ringing of the house-bell and she knew after all that Mr Mansfield had not come home. She listened a little longer, heard the house-bell a second and then a third time and at last looked through the canopy of apple-leaves to see, twenty yards or so away, a strange man of thirty-four or five admiring the wall of yellow roses, all curdling brilliance in the sun.

'Good afternoon. Was there something you wanted?' The words were formed and spoken before she realized how impossible and ridiculous her situation in the apple tree might seem. 'I'm up here. In the tree.'

Strongly featured, with a full mouth and dark hair and eyes, the man came across the lawn to the apple tree.

'Oh! there you are. Mrs Mansfield? I couldn't see you at first. You were quite hidden by leaves.'

'Yes, here I am.' It suddenly seemed necessary, for some reason, to explain her presence in the tree. 'I'm gathering a few apples.'

He smiled, cocking his head to one side in the way that birds sometimes do, half listening, half suspicious.

'Apples? I can't say they look very large.'

'Oh! no, no. I mean I'm merely thinning them out.'

'Oh! I see.'

He smiled again and she thought the vivacity of the dark eyes seemed very slightly mocking.

'Was there something you wanted? I'll come down.'

'Oh! no. Please don't.' He glanced swiftly and fully at her, perched up in the heart of the tree with her knees partly exposed against a branch, as if he frankly liked the sight of her in her light cream dress against the mass of shadow. 'I really wondered if Mr Mansfield was at home?'

'No. I'm expecting him. I thought in fact it was him when I heard you coming.'

'It's nothing desperate. It's just about an insurance paper.'

'I see.'

He looked at her openly again and once more with the sort of smile that seemed to mock her slightly. Uneasy, she held the edges of her dress tightly in her fingers.

He looked at his watch.

'How soon are you expecting him?'

'Oh! any moment. He's always down on the six-eight train.'

Again, and once more with the faintest mockery, he looked at his watch a second time.

'Six-eight? It isn't half past five.'

She felt herself flushing; like a girl she plunged into a vortex of hot embarrassment, her lips innocently quivering, her sudden rush of words unrelated to anything rational. She started to say stupidly:

'Oh! yes I know – I ought to have known. I mistook the time. But it really seemed later when I started to hide – '

'Started to what?'

With a smile that was really deadly serious he held her transfixed. In another and still more acute rush of embarrassment she could think of nothing to say but:

'I think I'll come down after all. All right, I can jump – '

'Don't jump. For God's sake,' he said. 'You'll break a leg.'

With a springing sort of gesture he held up both arms. A moment later, hardly conscious in the depths of her embarrassment of doing it, she half slid, half dropped from the tree. He caught her under the armpits and she was conscious of a narrow dart of pain rushing up like an ecstatic arrow through the centre of her body as her feet touched the ground.

'I once jumped out of a tree and broke a leg,' he said. 'I wouldn't want you to go through that pain.'

The way he said this seemed to her very personal; his voice was completely serious. Then something made her say:

'They always say men can't bear pain. But I must confess I'm not very good at it myself.'

'The gnawing of the bone when it knits,' he said, 'God, I'll never forget that. I can still feel it sometimes when I dream. I feel the actual pain.'

'You dream a lot?'

'Rather. Yes: often.'

'In colour?'

She did not know what made her ask this; all her thoughts were unpremeditated.

'Yes, I do. Now you come to ask, quite often in colour.'

'How extraordinary.'

'Extraordinary. Why?'

'It's very rare for a man to dream in colour. Women often do. But not men.'

'Oh?' he said. Now his voice was sceptical. He looked at her again in that bird-like, sideways, softly mocking way. 'How do you know? Do you ask people whether they – '

'Oh! no, no, no.' Confusion made her face redden again. She looked hopelessly shy. 'I read all about it somewhere in an article. It said it was a fact – it was very, very rare for men.'

'I must be a freak, then.' He laughed a warm, friendly laugh, head thrown back. 'Does Mr Mansfield dream in colour?'

'Mr Mansfield? Oh! I wouldn't know about that.'

'Wouldn't know?'

'Well, you see, I – Oh! I've never asked him. I wouldn't know if he even dreams.'

'How odd.'

'Odd? Yes, I suppose it is – but then you see, we don't – we have – I mean, we always – '

A great rush of confusion overtook her again. Just as she had no idea why she should suddenly start discussing dreams with an entire stranger so she now had no idea what odd new words were coming next. Incredibly she said:

'What I mean is – you see, we have separate rooms. We always – '

She broke off, but the flight of the remaining few unspoken words had already reached their destination as surely as if she had uttered them.

That's Mr Mansfield's way of keeping me on a throne – the thought went crazily whirling through her head like an accusing flagellation – the Princess. Me, Prinny. Gracious Heaven, what on earth am I thinking?

'I had a marvellously clear dream in colour one night last week. Clear as paint,' he said. 'Oh! I'm sorry I didn't introduce myself. Here we stand talking and – my name's George Seamark. I work for Lister's. I met Mr Mansfield on the train the other day and we got talking. He's arranging an insurance policy for me.'

'I see. What was the dream?'

'Oh! beautiful. I dreamed I caught a golden oriole. You know, it's a bird.'

'Oh?' she said. 'I don't think I know it.' She paused for quite some moments, remembering with irritation Mr Mansfield and the thrush. 'What does it look like?'

'Yellow. A lovely golden yellow.'

'I don't think I ever saw one.'

'Oh! you wouldn't. Not in this country: it isn't a native. One or two sometimes migrate here in the summer, but – '

'And you caught it in your hands?'

'Picked it up off the ground. Just like that. Quite tame.' He laughed lightly. 'Oh! and another extraordinary thing. It spoke to me.'

'Really? What did it say?'

'Just its name. Oriole. That's all. Oriole.' He laughed again. 'And then of course I woke up.'

She too felt suddenly as if she were waking up. An extraordinary dream had unwoven itself in the short distance between the apple tree and the rose on the house wall. The heat of the evening sun extracted from the mass of golden petals a deep and drugging sweetness and she drew a great breath of it, momentarily shutting her eyes and then opening them again.

When she consciously looked about her, fully awake as it were, it was to see Mr Mansfield, brief-case in hand, padding flabbily up the drive.

'Ah! young Seamark. I thought it looked like you. Brought the papers, I suppose. Remember your birth certificate?'

'Damn.'

'Never mind. Give it to me tomorrow morning on the train.'

'I'm not going up tomorrow. I'll have to drop it in – I'll try to remember it tomorrow afternoon.'

'Will you stay and have a cup of tea?' Mrs Mansfield said. 'Oh! it's no trouble. I'm going to get some for Mr Mansfield anyway.'

'Oh! yes – stay. Prinny will soon get it,' Mr Mansfield said. 'I'm dying for a cup. The heat on that train!'

Mrs Mansfield started to walk away to the house. As she turned towards the wall of petals the intense concentration of gold so momentarily dazzled her that when, at the doorway, something made her turn and look back she saw the two men almost as two tremulous ghosts, dream-bound and unreal, in a haze.

A few moments later she was hiding away in the kitchen – only this time not from Mr Mansfield but in some strange way from herself.

A curious premonition made her put the kettle on to boil, the following afternoon, at half past three. Two minutes later

George Seamark, birth certificate in hand, walked up the drive.

'I thought tomato sandwiches would be cool,' she said as she poured tea behind the drawn blinds of the sitting-room. 'It's awfully hot again.'

The unguarded innocence of the remark was not lost on George Seamark, who suddenly realized that she had been expecting him.

'The temperature didn't even seem to drop in the night,' she said. 'I couldn't sleep at all. In fact I came down and wandered around in the garden for a time.'

'Slept like a top,' he said. 'I was tired. Not a sign of a dream either.'

She was wearing a sleeveless dress of very pale blue, open at the neck for coolness, that exaggerated the air of innocence, almost girlish, that always hung about her. The skin of her rather long bare arms was creamy in tone. The pale wide eyes were almost transparent. But it was really the extraordinary pristine smoothness of the shoulders and arms that struck George Seamark with increasing fascination. It was not merely unblemished; it gave the impression of never having been touched before.

George Seamark ate six or seven tomato sandwiches and drank two cups of tea and they talked for a time of trivialities. Then he said at last:

'I suppose I'll have to get used to this heat. Going to get plenty of it in my new job.'

'New job?'

'Lister's are sending me to Amman. They've got a huge new contract there. It's quite a step up. That's why I took out the insurance.'

She felt she wanted to say something like 'How nice for you. Congratulations,' but she suddenly felt a peculiar coldness in the cavity of her heart again and said:

'How soon do you go?'

'I fly out in three weeks.'

'Oh! my goodness that isn't long.'

'Long enough. I've had a month's leave to pack.'

'A whole month? Really?'

She spoke as if it were a matter of personal concern. At the same time, quite unaware of it, she threw up her hands. When they fell again the long arms seemed to droop.

The gesture aroused George Seamark to a realization that the arms were very beautiful. The soft underparts of them quivered softly. Later, when she got up to pour tea, she bent over the table and he saw the same unblemished softness in the upper line of her breasts. Everything about her had the pristine mould of a girl.

Now he remembered something.

'I hope you won't think I'm being very personal,' he said. 'But what was it Mr Mansfield called you yesterday? Pinny?'

'Oh! no, no.' She tried to laugh lightly but sucked at her lip instead. 'Prinny. Not Pinny.'

'Oh! I see. I didn't quite catch it.'

'It's really rather silly.'

'Oh! I'm sorry.'

'Oh! it isn't that I mind.'

Neither of them spoke for a few moments. She lifted the lid of the teapot and looked inside it. She needed, she thought, to fetch some more hot water.

'I suppose married people often have silly names for each other. Just like children. Are you married, by the way?'

'Escaped so far.'

'Escaped? You think it might be an escape?'

'Not really. Plenty of time yet, that's all.'

She laughed, this time with relief. 'I just thought you might be one of those men who go about pretending that all women are insufferable –'

'Oh! Good Lord, no. I'm gone on them.'

She picked up the teapot, nervous now. The inner fold of her crooked arm, with its shadowy division of the flesh, all at once struck George Seamark as being like the soft hollow

between two breasts and he had a sudden powerful impulse
to catch it and hold it in his hand.

'Let me take the teapot.'

'Oh! no, I can manage it. I won't be a moment. Please have
something else to eat, won't you?'

He followed her into the kitchen. The shadowy hollow of
the crooked arm as she lifted the kettle from the stove once
again obsessed him while he stood a yard or two away,
watching.

'I told you I could manage – '

'Prinny,' he said. 'That isn't right for you. How did that
come about?'

'I told you, it's awfully silly. Why did you come into the
kitchen?'

She was about to pick up the teapot; instead she let her hands
fall to her sides. The very flatness of her attitude merely
heightened the habitual pristine innocence, embalming her in a
state of apparently appalled wonder.

'I wanted to be near you.'

'Near me? Why?'

He slipped his hand into the crook of her arm. The blood
throbbed up from the pulse fiercely. He let his hand travel
slowly up the arm until it reached the armpit and then the apple
of the shoulder and as he did so she gave something like the
beginnings of a protesting cry.

'Prinny,' he said. 'Prinny. How ever did that come about?'

'It was just that he called me a princess once. That's all.
That's how it began.'

'Princess. I understand that. That's more like it.'

He pressed his mouth against the side of her face. Immediately
she gave a convulsive start and began to turn away.

'You shouldn't do that. It's not right to do that.'

'Not right?' he said. 'Why not right? Just because he
doesn't do it?'

With something like anguish she lifted both arms in a lost,
erratic sort of gesture and held her head in her hands.

'Oh! my God,' she said, 'Oh! my God, don't confuse me. Don't confuse me, please.'

She was walking in the garden the following afternoon when, about four o'clock, she suddenly saw him coming up the drive. Almost as if she had mistaken him for Mr Mansfield she hurriedly hid herself behind a large syringa bush in full white bloom. She stood there for almost five minutes, holding her breath and trembling and hearing the house-bell ring.

Shortly after this, out of curiosity, George Seamark strolled into the garden and she was at once in the ridiculous situation of not knowing whether to reveal herself or to stay hidden until, as with Mr Mansfield, she was discovered. She stood trapped in a mortal agony of embarrassment, made worse by the thick heavy perfume of syringa, exquisite at any time but now so overpowering that it was almost like a drug.

Presently she knew by the sound of his footsteps that he was coming towards her. A violent and ill-controlled impulse to run away had the effect of suddenly making her swivel her whole body round in a full circle, so that she felt positively faint for a moment or two and almost overbalanced as she turned.

Then he was there, by the syringa bush, staring at her. She was still trembling so much that in pure fear of being seen she whipped her hands behind her back exactly as if she were concealing something from him.

When he spoke at last it was very slowly, in a whisper.

'You were hiding from me. Didn't you want to see me today?'

'It wasn't that.'

'You were hiding, weren't you?'

'Yes.'

She too was speaking in a whisper.

'Why?'

She paused for several seconds, biting her lip.

'I don't know. I can't tell you.'

'You're not afraid of me, are you?'

'Oh! no, no. Oh! dear, no.'

'Was it because of what I did yesterday?'

'Not exactly. Well, partly perhaps, yes.'

'But I didn't do anything yesterday really, did I? I simply touched you, that's all.'

Before speaking again she gave him a look of desperate appeal, hopelessly at a loss, her face almost as white as the great mass of syringa blossom behind her.

'I told you before, these things are very confusing to someone like me.'

'You mean just because I touched your arm?'

'It wasn't only that. You said you came into the kitchen because you wanted to be near me.' She looked at him again with an appeal so painful that it magnified her habitual air of innocence into something so manifestly complicated that her now flushed face actually seemed twisted. 'But don't you see? – you've only known me such a little while! Only a few minutes –'

He made as if to take her by both arms and then, sharply aware of all the acuteness of her embarrassment, thought better of it and said:

'There are people you want to touch the first time you ever see them. Haven't you ever felt like that?'

'I can't say that I have.'

'It's often happened to me,' he said. 'I was in a café once, having tea. I had an awful impulse to touch the waitress's arm while she served me. I suppose she might not have minded but I couldn't stand it. I had to go out –'

'You're a real man,' she said with sudden and almost violent bitterness. 'Choked with vanity. I suppose she might not have minded! –'

'I didn't mean it quite like that.'

'No? It sounded as if you made a habit of going round touching women for fun. Or perhaps it's just at tea-time that it comes over you?'

This last remark, exactly like something delivered by a vexed and sarcastic schoolgirl, made him smile. She lacked the necessary experience to answer his quiet 'Really now?' or, for a moment or two, his sudden change of subject:

'You still haven't told me why you were hiding from me.'

'Do I have to tell you? It's a very personal matter.'

'So is dreaming in colour.'

'Yes: I asked you about that, didn't I?'

He held her for nearly half a minute in a full gaze, not speaking. The particular warm whiteness of the great mass of syringa blossom had seemed for the last few moments to give her face an exceptionally dark flush but now the blood drained suddenly away again, leaving her mouth pale.

'Do you hide a lot?' he said. 'You were hiding in the apple tree the other day.'

The unexpected mention of the apple tree was more than she could bear. With another helpless look of twisted bewilderment she murmured something about how hot it was and how she would have to go into the house, out of the sun.

A moment later she started to walk uncertainly up the path towards the house and he followed her. Another afternoon of torrid heat had seared the edges of many of the yellow roses on the house wall. The scalded petals were dropping fast. Whole roses were bursting and falling like over-ripened fruits and as she walked towards the door a sudden uplift of air brought down a flocking yellow shower of petals, many of them settling on her hair.

The effect of such brilliant sunlight was so great that in the dark shade of the passage inside the house the two of them were temporarily blinded. She actually stopped and groped with her hands. George Seamark stopped too and for a few seconds all he could distinguish with any clarity at all were the petals that had fallen like so many golden yellow shells on her hair.

Most of them were still there when he and Mrs Mansfield reached the kitchen. In the stronger light, as she instinctively reached out for the kettle, he thought how beautiful the petals looked and once again, excited, he caught her by the crook of her arm.

'You're all covered with yellow petals,' he said. 'All over your hair.'

The tension was so great in her that she was completely unable to speak; she could only stare at him in absorbed and pristine wonder.

'Almost like a golden oriole.'

A moment later, holding her by the bare upper arm, he was kissing her for the first time.

It might have been thought that this first wholly intimate act between them would have had a disruptive and shattering effect on her but she afterwards confessed that it achieved an entirely opposite state of things. It fell on her like a great hush; it created in her a state of blissful and beautiful inertia, a great vacuum of calm.

Nor did the departure of George Seamark an hour or so later do anything to break it. It was exactly as if, at last, she had found somewhere inside herself a supremely secure and perfect hiding-place.

'I'll come and see you every afternoon I can before I go away.'

'Is that wise? I'm sure the neighbours all have telescopes.'

'Then we'll drive out in the car.'

'That still isn't very wise.'

'Then you could walk to meet me somewhere and I can pick you up.'

'Yes, I could do that. You can take me out to the woods. No one will see us there.'

'Supposing it should rain?'

'On rainy days you can come here.'

It was a week before the weather broke. An afternoon storm of torrential violence suddenly turned the sky to smoke and washed George Seamark up against the door of the Mansfield house as against a breakwater, half-drowned.

'You should have brought an umbrella.'

'Umbrellas are very dangerous in thunderstorms. Besides, it was quite fine when I started.'

'You're absolutely soaked. It's even gone through to your shirt.'

'Don't worry about the shirt. Kiss me.'

'You're too wet to be kissed. I can't get near you. I'll spoil my dress.'

'Then take your dress off.'

'Take my dress off? What an extraordinary thing to suggest.'

'What's extraordinary about it?'

They were standing in the passage where, on an earlier occasion, he had been so blinded by sunlight that it had been for a few moments impossible to see anything but the glint of yellow petals. Now he could see her better. The pristine innocence of the large blue eyes was not merely startled; it almost erupted with shock.

He took off his rain-soaked jacket and hung it on a hat peg. Streams of water from his drenched clothing were running down and forming little pools on the mosaic of the passage floor. In a jocular sort of voice he murmured something about how he would certainly have to undress pretty soon even if she herself had other views about it and she said, again completely startled:

'Well, of course you'll have to. But not in front of me, I hope.'

'Why not in front of you? It wouldn't embarrass me.'

'But it would embarrass me. Terribly.'

'Why?'

'Well, I should think it just would, that's all.'

'Kiss me. I love you. I'm very, very wet and I love you.'

'You're very very wet and I think you're mocking me.'

'Mock you? I wouldn't mock you for all the wide world.'

In another moment he was holding her, pressing his rain-soaked body full against the front of her dress. He kissed her for a long time, recreating once again inside her the deep and blissful inertia that was like soundless vacuum. Locked away, when the kiss was over, she heard him whisper the incredible suggestion, as it seemed from a great distance, almost from some hiding-place of his own:

'Undress for me. Undress for me, will you, this afternoon?'

In an inertia now utterly complete she stood quite speechless.

'Undress for me.'

If he had suddenly jabbed her with a knife he could hardly have aroused a greater look of vacuous horror than he saw on her face a moment later.

'Please.'

Still unable to speak, she merely shook her head in reply.

'I'm going away soon. There won't be much more time.'

Not even looking at him, she could only shake her head again.

'Undress for me.'

'Please! – do you know what you're asking me?'

'It's very simple. I'll be very tender with you. You needn't be afraid.'

'It isn't that.'

In a whisper, his mouth close to her face, he asked her what she meant by this. She turned her face sharply, incapable of looking at him, and a second later a shock of infinite astonishment went through him too.

'I've never undressed in front of anyone in my life before.'

As she said this she looked almost frightened. He held her closely against him, her head hidden against his wet shoulders.

A moment later she suddenly broke away from him and started to run upstairs. The old instinct to hide herself was in action before she was aware of it.

Some time later he found her in her bedroom, half hidden by a curtain. She had drawn the window-blinds. Rain was pouring on the windows and this was the only sound except her sharply indrawn breath as he put his hands on her shoulders.

'Why did you draw the blinds?'

'I just felt as if a great crowd of eyes were watching me.'

'I'm the only one that's watching you.'

'I know. You'll think I'm silly, but I'm afraid of that too.'

'There's no need to be afraid.'

'I suppose not. No, I suppose there isn't any need.'

Then she confessed two things. The first was that since he had first kissed her there had been this great calmness inside her; she had existed in an indescribably beautiful vacuum. The second was that she couldn't sleep at nights: not after the usual restless way of insomnia, but simply out of happiness. It was like being under a celestial sort of spell.

'I'm happy for the first time in my life, I think. I don't want to sleep. I don't want to sleep for fear of missing any of it.'

'I must say I don't sleep very well either.'

'I came down and walked in the garden last night. It was still marvellously warm. There were glow-worms. You only see them in very hot weather.'

'I've never seen one.'

'Perhaps you'll see them in Amman. Golden orioles by day and glow-worms by night. That would be nice for you.'

He started gently to stroke her shoulders.

'That was something I've got to talk to you about. Amman.'

'Yes?'

'It seems they want me to go out quite a bit earlier. I'll be flying the day after tomorrow.'

'Oh!'

'That was why I wanted you to undress for me.'

'Please. Not today. Let me think about it. But not today.'

Presently he stopped stroking her shoulders and put his two hands under her breasts. They were as firm and unrelaxed as a young girl's and he lifted them slightly with the tips of his fingers. A state of great wonder enveloped her as he did this and in the partially shaded room her eyes seemed larger and clearer than ever.

'I know you find it hard to believe all this. But no one has ever done that to me before.'

'Undress for me.'

'Not now. Not today. Oh! it isn't because I think it's wrong or anything like that.'

'Then what is it?'

She said a strange thing in reply.

'I don't want it to happen deliberately, that's all. I want it to happen like a discovery.'

That night, sleepless once more, she slipped a light dressing wrap over her nightgown and went downstairs and walked about the garden. It was nearly midnight and quite dark and the heavy rain had stopped some hours before. The grass of the lawn was quite dry again already but there were no signs of glow-worms and she kept telling herself that the rain had washed them all away.

'No glow-worms tonight?'

The voice of George Seamark was lowered to a whisper.

'Oh! my God, how you frightened me.'

He took hold of her hand without another word and they walked across the lawn and then stood under the apple tree where he had first discovered her hiding. He slipped the wrap from her shoulders and then undid the frontal ribbon of her nightdress. In the darkness she stood absolutely motionless and, completely unafraid now, let him make his discovery.

'You remember young Seamark,' Mr Mansfield said. It was more than three months later and occasionally, already, the September nights were growing chilly. A small second flush of yellow roses now graced the house wall and all about the garden apples were big and colouring to ripeness. 'Strangest thing happened about him. It seems they decided to send him home.'

'Oh?'

'Seems he no sooner got out there than he picked up a bug. He started to have queer fainting fits apparently. For no reason at all he'd suddenly just fall down.'

'No reason at all?'

'Decided to send him home by ship. I rather think they

thought the long air-trip would be too much for him and the sea voyage might do him good.'

'Is he home?'

'He just disappeared one night on the ship,' Mr Mansfield said. 'Seems he didn't sleep very well and went on deck to get some air. A steward saw him leaning on the rail.'

'Oh?'

'No doubt he must have had one of those fainting fits and overbalanced and – Oh! of course we shall pay. The circumstances are a bit odd but we shall pay. I discussed it with head office. It upset me when I heard. I liked that young man. I rather think you liked him too, didn't you?'

'Yes, I quite liked him. He was rather fond of birds.'

'Fond of birds?'

A sudden impulse to start running died in her, leaving her body gripped by a great chill. She experienced a hopeless fit of shuddering and tried to control it by wringing her hands together.

'Fancy that,' Mr Mansfield said. 'Fond of birds? I wish I'd known. We might have had a talk together. We might have found we sort of had things in common.'

'I don't think so.'

'No? What makes you say that?'

'Well in a way he wasn't interested in birds. Not the birds you see here, I mean. They were rather the sort of birds you dream of – '

Mr Mansfield said he didn't understand. The strong impulse to start running woke in her again but she checked it and started to walk into the garden instead. She walked with a sort of drifting slowness, shuddering again, and when she reached the centre of the lawn she suddenly stopped, threw her arms crosswise about her chest and shoulders and stared wildly about her.

It was as if she had found herself suddenly naked and had no way of hiding any longer.

# Mr Featherstone Takes a Ride

Within a minute of catching the two cockerels from the pen in the field Niggler hopped back over the fence and was deftly wringing their necks with a croaky, cheerful laugh that was like an echo of the voices of the expiring birds. In another minute they were safely in the back of the two-ton truck drawn up by the side of the chestnut wood.

'Could have been a bit plumper. Don't give 'em enough corn,' Niggler said in a rather injured sort of way. 'Still they'll roast nice and tender.'

Mr Featherstone, who had something of the look of a frightened, pale and studious giraffe, sat trembling in the driving cab. He seemed about to melt in the heat of sheer nervousness. As a student he had hitched lifts often enough before; but he really wasn't used to this sort of thing.

'What ever are you doing?' Mr Featherstone's tremulous voice had a slight stammer. 'Why can't we get going?'

To his despairing astonishment Niggler had lifted the bonnet of the lorry and was already sunk in calm consultation with the engine, oblivious of the slight spring rain that had started to fall.

'We'll have someone see us,' Mr Featherstone said. He pleaded desperately: 'Please. For goodness' sake let's go.'

'Carburettor.'

Niggler, with brown, oily hands, casually caressed the carburettor as if about to dally with it in a dreamy sort of way. His voice was oily too. His sharp blue eyes seemed to be made of cut-glass as they flashed to and fro between carburettor and the quavering Mr Featherstone and once they gave a positive wink of confidence that almost clicked aloud.

'Been pulling bad all the way along. Probably got some muck in it. Might have to take it down.'

'But surely not here?' Mr Featherstone said. 'For Heaven's sake.' He turned desperately to look about him and was instantly dismayed to see the figure of a man in heavy green sweater and gum-boots hurriedly approaching across the field where the hens and cockerels were. There was clearly something menacing in its haste and Mr Featherstone felt his heart give several sickening turns. 'For the Lord's sake let's get going. There's a man coming across the field.'

'Oh?' Niggler said. 'Where?'

Placidly he lifted a face that might at some time have been partly flattened by a mighty blow. The big nose had been crushed to the shape of a pear crudely cut in half. The mouth was like a purse emptied of its contents and left loosely open in a big, good-natured leer. The whole thing was so manifestly distorted that it was in a fascinating and compulsive sort of way quite handsome.

'Farmer, I expect.' With a spanner Niggler made a few casual, impressive adjustments to the carburettor. 'Bloke what keeps the cockerels I expect.'

'Kept,' Mr Featherstone said. 'Kept. My God –'

Presently the man in the gum-boots, who was carrying two letters in his hand, was exchanging friendly greetings; but Mr Featherstone, who now felt slightly faint, discovered he had no voice with which to answer them.

'Coming on for a wet evening. Hope it won't come on too fast before I get to the post. Trouble?'

'Nothing much.' Coolly Niggler lowered the bonnet, shutting it with as much care, very slowly, as if it had been made of eggshell. 'Carburettor. Gets out of kilter on these long runs.'

'Going far?'

As far as possible, Mr Featherstone's mind chattered, as far as possible.

'Make Salisbury tonight,' Niggler said. 'No hurry.' Mr Featherstone sat in the cab with closed eyes, feeling himself growing rapidly fainter and fainter. 'All done to schedule.'

'Ah well. Hope it clears up for you.'

'Hope so too. Looking forward to a good dinner.' Mr Featherstone, given strength, could have groaned. Instead he merely sat in a pretence of sleep, listening in sickened astonishment to a further casual statement from Niggler, who stood carefully rolling a cigarette, slowly licking the paper with a big flannelly tongue. 'Your cockerels are a bit near the road, mate. Foxes ever get any? I mean the two-legged kind?'

'Can't say they have done yet.'

'What made me ask,' Niggler said, 'was two chaps in a Ford Zephyr who was parked here when we pulled up.' He raised his voice to a cheerful, matey call that almost had Mr Featherstone falling out of the cab. 'Wasn't they, Mr Feather?'

In a strange low voice that didn't belong to him Mr Featherstone started to agree that he thought there had been something of the kind and at the same time opened his eyes to see Niggler actually buttonholing the man in gum-boots with an air of supreme confidence, as if in the act of doing him a good turn.

'They nipped off too smart for my liking,' Niggler said. 'I get to know the good 'uns and the bad 'uns driving up and down these roads, I tell you. One of 'em come out of the wood with a bag.'

'Well, thanks for the tip –'

'They went that way,' Niggler said. He was half-way up into the cab, pointing with his free hand back down the road. 'They went like grease lightning round the corner. I said they'd bleedin' cop it round the corner if they didn't watch out. Didn't I, Mr Feather? You said so too, didn't you?'

In barely audible murmurs Mr Featherstone agreed that he thought they would certainly cop it. Nor, he thought desperately, will they be the only ones.

Niggler started the engine. Prayerfully Mr Featherstone had just begun to think 'Thank God!' when Niggler leaned cheerfully from the cab to impart several more expansive pieces of information to the man in gum-boots.

'Mr Feather's a student. Going right the way to Penzance. Got an aunt there. Nice company for me all the way.'

Niggler pushed in the gear-lever and then decided that his cigarette wasn't burning too well and pushed back into neutral again. A smell of rank shag filled the air. Mr Featherstone closed his eyes again and as in a dream heard a feeble cock-crow from the field that suddenly filled him with the odious nightmare that the cockerels in the back of the lorry had somehow reincarnated themselves and were giving warning cries of their true plight there.

'Well, so long.' These, Mr Featherstone thought as he heard the gear-lever grate in again, were the most blessed words of his life and he actually felt the lorry moving forward. Then it stopped, the cause being that Niggler had one final, cheerful confidential piece of information to impart.

He imparted it with thumb up:

'I just remembered. I took the number of that car: EKΘ 461 it was.'

Some hours later, as it seemed, Mr Featherstone woke from an uneasy, shag-drugged doze. Spring rain was falling in tiny beads on the windscreen and through the arcs made by the windscreen wipers he could see open chalky stretches of downland dotted about with occasional greening beech trees. Niggler was humming some disconnected snatches of a pop tune and driving into the gentle rain at a steady thirty-five.

An immediate spasm of guilt made Mr Featherstone look back through the window of the cab to see if the truck was being followed but Niggler put an end to any speculation of that sort by asking in his ebullient off-hand way how Mr Featherstone liked his chicken done?

'I like mine with stuffing,' Niggler said.

The thought of chicken, let alone stuffing, brought sharp prickles of nausea to Mr Featherstone's throat. Niggler, oblivious of any idea that the conversation might be giving pain, licked his lips with a meaty smack. He liked plenty of onion stuffing, he told Mr Featherstone, and nice bread sauce.

In a weakened, neutral voice Mr Featherstone found himself asking:

'How much farther is Salisbury?'

'About fifteen. Ought to be there about six.'

'I think I shall say good-bye to you at Salisbury.'

Niggler, with something like reproach, said he wouldn't hear of it. It was a bleedin' long way to Penzance yet. Besides, they were going to kip at Salisbury and have dinner there. Wasn't that all right?

'Well, actually – '

'Actually what?' Niggler said. He was deftly rolling another cigarette, one-handed. 'I got some nice friends there. Two old ladies. I often kip there. Don't cost a penny.'

'Well, it's very kind of you, but – '

'But what?'

Mr Featherstone had to confess to himself that he didn't know. He had less than fifteen shillings in his pocket and the fare to Penzance alone would have been more than four pounds. It wasn't always easy hitching lifts in the rain either. A cheap dinner and a free bed would save him a lot.

'The dinner won't cost nothing neither,' Niggler said. 'The old ladies'll cook it. Or rather I shall.'

Mr Featherstone, stammering, started to feel oppressively faint again.

'You don't mean to say that somebody else is going to be involved in those chickens?'

''Course they're involved. That's what I got 'em for. I always try to take 'em a couple. Or a brace of pheasants sometimes. Or a goose.'

Mr Featherstone sat quiet, simply watching the hills, the windscreen wipers and the rain.

'Like a fag?' Niggler said. 'I can roll another.'

With a stammering politeness Mr Featherstone rejected the offer of a fag. Niggler, with customary deftness, lit up again, filling the air with monstrous fog.

A second or two later Niggler was addressing Mr

Featherstone in tones of inoffensive reproach, almost a lecture:

'I believe you're a bit worried about them cockerels. Well, you don't want to be. They're doing somebody a good turn. It's just a kind act, see? When you see them two old ladies sucking on the bones you'll understand, see? You'll see real happiness.'

'But you say you do it regularly,' Mr Featherstone protested. 'Aren't you ever afraid of getting caught?'

'You'll see real happiness,' Niggler said. 'Real proper happiness. It'll do your heart good.'

Mr Featherstone, half-asphyxiated, felt curiously chastened and could think of nothing to say. Niggler puffed heavily at shag, eyes half-closed against the smoke's bitter tang.

'By the way, what do you study? What are you a student of, I mean?' Niggler gave a rousing, shag-choked guffaw. 'Form?'

'Form?'

'The horses. The gee-gees. Don't follow the gee-gees?'

Mr Featherstone said he was afraid not. He couldn't afford to follow the gee-gees. He hadn't the cash to spare. No: he was a student of philosophy.

'What does that mean exactly?'

Well, it was hard to explain in simple terms, Mr Featherstone said.

'Not birds, is it?'

'No, no. That's ornithology.'

'Studying this means going to college, I reckon?'

University, Mr Featherstone explained. Oxford. He thought a few moments longer in silence and then said:

'I've been trying to think of the proper definition of philosophy. I think I've got it more or less right. I suppose it would go something like this: it's the love of wisdom; in actual usage, the knowledge of phenomena as explained by, and resolved into, causes and reasons, powers and laws.'

A stunned silence greeted Mr Featherstone's words. The fag almost dropped from Niggler's lips.

'Of course that's the merest essence of it,' Mr Featherstone went on. 'In a narrow sense it's almost the equivalent of meta-physics, but usually it's understood as also including all the mental and moral sciences such as logic, psychology, ethics, and so on.'

'Blimey.'

'Of course there are all sorts of sections, or used to be. Natural philosophy for example – '

'Does it do any good?'

'Well, it really isn't a question of doing good. Philosophy really denotes a systematic body of general conceptions – '

'Yes, but blimey, what's it *for*?'

By now Niggler's fag had gone completely out. Utterly unable to carry the conversation further he too stared blindly at hills, windscreen wipers, and rain. Presently the fag actually dropped from his lips and Mr Featherstone said in a matter-of-fact tone of voice that he would try to put the whole thing into simpler, more fundamental terms.

'Take for instance you. What do you reckon life is made up of? I mean how do you yourself see it? People, I mean. What sort of categories do people seem to you to fall into?'

Niggler came sharply to life with a spontaneous laugh, full of sudden understanding and cheerful gusto.

'Only two,' he said. 'Mugs and those who ain't.'

'Well, that,' Mr Featherstone said, 'is your philosophy.'

'It is?'

'Then take Hitler.'

Niggler, affronted, visibly recoiled, as if he greatly resented being bracketed with Hitler.

'The bastard,' he said.

'Hitler's philosophy,' Mr Featherstone went on, 'could be described as a Machiavellian one. Unlike Aristotle, who – '

'Mackiwhat?'

'Machiavellian,' Mr Featherstone proceeded to explain. 'Machiavelli was a Florentine diplomat and statesman who thought that any means, however unscrupulous or lawless, were justified in order to establish strong governmental power. The same could be said of Khrushchev – '

'Another rum 'un,' Niggler said. 'The big fat frog.'

Mr Featherstone stammered on, warming up. He invited an astonished Niggler to consider Aristotle. It was generally held that Aristotle was the greatest of all philosophical thinkers. He was in a sense the father of it all. Dante, for instance, had called him 'the master of those who know'. His first principle had been adopted from one of Plato – that of the self activity of an intelligent first cause of all. On the other hand –

Stunned to a new and deeper silence, Niggler could only roll another fag. He rolled it like a man in a dream and finally let it dangle from his pouchy lips unlit. This silence lasted for a full five minutes, at the end of which he came to himself to hear Mr Featherstone say:

'That was the sign for Salisbury. We must be nearly there.'

Niggler immediately cast quick, irritated eyes about the landscape, cursing, as if unable to believe he was actually where he was.

'Gawd blimey, Feather, you gone and made me overshoot the bleedin' turning. It's a bleedin' mile back there.'

'I'm most terribly sorry,' Mr Featherstone said. 'I'd really no idea.'

With every lock of the wheel as he turned the truck round Niggler cursed good-naturedly, saying finally:

'Mustn't overshoot the old ladies. They're expectin' me. I promised 'em the cockerels last week.'

'You mean you actually planned that business? It wasn't a sudden impulse?'

'Gawd blimey, no. I always plan it. I note 'em comin' one way and nick 'em goin' the other. Don't believe in impulses, Feather. They scare me.'

With this philosophical touch Niggler gave one of his stentorian croaky laughs and finally lit the fag. Fresh clouds of shag smoke filled the air so thickly that it was suddenly impossible to see out of the cab and Niggler was actually forced to stop for a minute and clean the windscreen with his sleeve.

Peering through the glass, he announced that the rain had

stopped and that it was going to be a fine spring evening after all. Thinking of the cockerels, he chuckled. Mr Featherstone's bewildering discourse on the philosophies was far behind him now. From now on it was chickens, stuffing and the old bread sauce.

'Look.' He nudged Mr Featherstone in the ribs, at the same time half blinding him with a positively volcanic eruption of shag. 'That's where we're going, Feather. In them gates. In there.'

A pair of rusting iron gates that might once have belonged to a palace of sorts were pushed back from two stone pillars surmounted by a pair of preening eagles, one of which had lost its head.

Through these and into a forest of long neglected laurel and rhododendron, everywhere entwined by brambles, Niggler drove the truck, explaining at the same time that it was here, on a late windy December afternoon, while changing a wheel, that he had first met the old ladies, Miss Montifiore and Miss Pearce.

'It was bleedin' mucky and cold. They took pity on me and asked me in for a cuppa and they bleedin' near hung me on the Christmas tree.'

At the end of the bramble-shrouded drive a house of indeterminate design, part Tudor, part Victorian, part Scottish baronial, rose from a square of thistle-infested lawn not unlike a forlorn terracotta memorial to some event long forgotten.

Half-way up the drive Niggler started sounding the horn, at the same time croaking with laughter so much that the fag dropped out of his mouth. He made no attempt to pick it up but instead invited Mr Featherstone, with enthusiastic cheerfulness, to look ahead.

Mr Featherstone did so and suddenly saw, on the gravel square in front of the house, as if in answer to Niggler's raucous signal on the horn, two female figures waving hands.

'Oh! Niggler, how absolutely thrilling to see you.'

Miss Montifiore, to whom Mr Featherstone presently found

himself being introduced, was pinkish, thin and supple, rather
like a stick of early rhubarb. Her movements were gracious;
her voice was full of high, piercing charm.

'Hullo, Niggler, you old so and so. How goes it, eh?
Good show.'

Miss Pearce, forthright, short and over-plump, was pudding-
like in her physical excesses. She was wearing slacks of dark
green corduroy and a white silk shirt with a golden tie. Her
bosom was of such curious, elongated shape that she seemed to
have been obliged to wrap the lower parts of it round her
waist. Her large face, with its oiled black hair brushed clean
back in masculine fashion, showed none of the distortions that
Niggler's bore. Instead it merely seemed that someone had
once blown it up too high with a pump and then forgotten to
let out the air.

'Oh! we don't live in the house,' Miss Montifiore said to Mr
Featherstone, who had felt constrained to make polite remarks aboot it. 'Couldn't possibly. Taxation wouldn't allow
that, even if we could get the servants, which we can't.'

It was about this time that Mr Featherstone noticed that
Miss Pearce always called her companion Monty and that she
in turn was called the Pearce.

'Got a flat over the stables,' the Pearce said. 'God, it's bloody
good to see you, Niggler.' The Pearce actually slapped him on
the back and then caught him one-handed, impulsively, in
a stout embrace. 'Going to kip with us for the night? Always
welcome, dear boy.'

Niggler thanked her with a 'Ta very much' and asked if
they'd had any more trouble with rats since he was here the
time before?

'None whatever,' Monty said. 'Your wonderful beer-trap
seems to have done the trick.'

'Beer-trap?' Mr Featherstone said. The four of them were
half-way to the stables now and he was brought up sharply.

'Niggler has invented this marvellous beer-trap,' the Pearce
explained. 'What he does or how we've no idea. For all I

know he may say incantations over the damn things, but the fact is they disappear.'

'I wasn't aware that rats liked beer,' Mr Featherstone said, suddenly coldly suspicious.

'Then you've never been inside a brewery,' Niggler said. 'You see 'em layin' about there drunk as newts.'

By the way, he went on to explain, Mr Feather was a student of philosophy on his way to Penzance. Was it all right if he kipped down too?

'Oh! the more the merrier,' the Pearce said. 'Any friend in Niggler's – by the way, did you ever see your little Fraül of Spiegler again? The Austrian girl you brought for the night? She was a student too, wasn't she? Pretty little thing. I rather fell for her.'

Niggler, ignoring all recollection of the pretty little Austrian thing, suddenly stopped and cursed loudly.

'Blast it. Forgot the cockerels.'

Mr Featherstone said he would go back for the cockerels and ten minutes later Niggler was at the kitchen sink, drawing and plucking them. Monty was laying the table for dinner and the Pearce was cutting up large creamy curds of broccoli, the last of the May Queens, she said. Mr Featherstone was sitting in an ancient wicker-chair, peeling potatoes.

'I'm afraid everyone here has to do a stint,' Monty said. 'You see, we get absolutely no help at all except Effie, who does the rough.'

All of a sudden the Pearce, engaged now in chopping parsley and onions for stuffing, let out a deep bark of inquiry, more masculine than any male.

'Dying to ask you, Niggler. What about the turf, dear boy? How did we fare?'

Niggler, busy cleaning up the birds, paused to say 'Ah! the horses. I got a note of 'em all somewhere. I'll get the stuffing in first though, and then we'll tot everything up.'

'You mean we *won*?'

Niggler gave one of his most spontaneous, croaky laughs.

'We always win, don't we?'

'Yes, I know we do. I know. But there's always the feeling we *must* come unstuck one day. You think we ever will?'

'I don't think so,' Niggler said. 'I don't think so.'

With bland and dexterous hands Niggler broke an egg into a basin and then proceeded to bind the stuffing with it. All the time Mr Featherstone turned on him a low, keen eye of suspicion but there was never a flicker of any kind in answer.

'You see,' the Pearce explained as she trimmed the rind off two pieces of streaky bacon, 'Niggler has this terrific flair about horses. Almost psychic. He's got a sort of genius for picking the right ones.'

Presently Niggler had finished stuffing the birds and soon they were in the oven, each with its neat brassière of bacon tied across the breast.

'Well now, let's have a butcher's,' Niggler said. An astonishing number of slips of paper fell from his wallet as he opened it. He selected one and for some time looked at it with studied penetration, as if seeking to interpret a text of some sort, at the same time scratching behind one ear.

'Oh! what *did* you do for us this week?' the Pearce said. 'I'm dying to know. That's what makes it so exciting – the not knowing part.'

'*Golden Rod*,' Niggler said. 'Seven-to-two. That never come up. *Bristol Fairy* – you had ten bob each way on that at eight-to-one. Fell down. *Crazy Night* – forty-to-one, I thought we had one there, but – Now let's see. That's right. *Son of Piper* – that come up at a hundred-to-nine. And *Fisherman's Song* – that came up at four-to-one.'

'Genius!' Monty said. 'Genius!'

'You damn well deserve half a chicken for yourself,' the Pearce said. 'What does that make us?'

Emerging presently from deep calculations Niggler said he reckoned it made them twenty-five bob apiece.

'And what,' said Mr Featherstone, 'did you lay out?'

'I think it was four pounds,' Monty said.

The outlay, Mr Featherstone remarked rather caustically, hardly seemed to justify the return, did it?

'Oh! on the contrary.' Monty suddenly seemed less rhubarb-like. She appeared to be fluffed up, almost affronted. 'I think it's amply, amply justified. The thrill alone. The excitement. We *adore* our little flutter.'

'In racing you've surely got to be philosophical,' the Pearce said. 'I should have thought that you, as a student of philosophy, would have known that.'

'Unfortunately I don't know very much about racing.'

'No?' the Pearce said, dealing Mr Featherstone a final, deeply crushing blow, 'and perhaps, by the same token, you don't know much about philosophy.'

Mr Featherstone was depressedly silent and Niggler, emerging not merely victorious but positively cosseted by the Pearce's words, said with a sudden sigh that he thought he could do with a glass of water.

'Oh! not water!' The two ladies almost exploded the words together. 'We have beer. We got a new crate in specially. Perhaps Mr Featherstone would like some too?'

Mr Featherstone rejected the idea of beer with polite thanks and said that he much preferred milk if there was any on hand.

'Mind if I smoke?' Niggler said and produced fag papers and shag, at the same time asking the Pearce if he could roll her one too. The Pearce thanked him but said she preferred her pipe, which she took out of her trousers pocket and tapped loudly on the heel of her shoe.

'Oh! the Pearce loves her pipe,' Monty said. 'Cigars too.'

'We'll have cigars after supper,' the Pearce said. 'We nearly always do when Niggler comes.'

As the fragrance of roasting chicken filled the air her resentments against Mr Featherstone seemed gradually to cool. She actually thanked him heartily for peeling the spuds – job she personally hated – and asked his opinion on how they should be done – plain boiled or roasted round the chicken?

'Both,' Niggler said. 'I'll do 'em. Leave 'em to me.'

'Marvellous man,' the Pearce said. 'Nothing he can't do. Niggler, where *did* you learn all these things?'

'Army cook,' Niggler said. 'Picked it all up there.'

'I shall never forget that delicious goose your friend let you have last autumn,' Monty said. 'That was a dream. You cooked it like an angel.'

Niggler, modest under the extravagant praise of the goose, puffed at his fag and stared hard at a newspaper, studying form.

'Now there's a nag here,' he started to say, 'what might do us a bit of all right –'

'Don't want to hear it!' the Pearce said. 'Don't want to hear it! Much prefer not to know. The thrill of the thing is not to know. It might easily break the spell if one knew.'

Airily Niggler waved a hand, conceding that perhaps the Pearce was right. What the eye didn't see the heart didn't grieve over.

'That's a true word,' Mr Featherstone said.

Niggler stared hard, almost as if hurt, at Mr Featherstone, who stood sipping milk and gazing out of the window at a mass of nettles invading what had once been a large rose-bed. The evening was delightful after all, with cuckoos still calling, and flies were dancing in the golden April air.

'Once we even had venison,' Monty said.

'Good God!' Mr Featherstone said. 'You mean you actually brought a deer?'

'Knocked it over with the lorry outside a big park,' Niggler said. 'I could hardly leave it dying there, could I?'

A combination of shag-smoke and that of mild fragrant flake now filled the air. The Pearce stood with trousered legs staunchly apart, puffing at her pipe, and asked Niggler heartily if it wasn't time the spuds were on? Niggler said he thought it was and got up to perform the necessary tasks, his fag dipping from one corner of his mouth, so that a cloud of ash fell smartly into the saucepan.

By half past eight, as the meal began, Niggler was well into his fourth pint of beer. The Pearce confessed several times that

she was dying of hunger and confided in Mr Featherstone
that it was only on the occasions of Niggler's visit that she and
Monty ever had a damn good blow-out like this.

'I can't cook an egg myself,' she said, 'and all Monty can
make is toad-in-the-hole.'

The two ladies and Mr Featherstone each had a glass of sherry
with the meal and immediately before the attack on the chickens
began the Pearce lifted her glass and said:

'Well, here's to your good friend who kindly lets us have
the chickens.'

'Here's to my friend,' Niggler said, studiously avoiding Mr
Featherstone's chilly eye, 'bless his heart.'

After that it was almost a free for all. Hungry as any trawler-
man on the high seas, Mr Featherstone pronounced in a
simmering stammer of enthusiasm that the food was frightfully, frightfully good. He congratulated Niggler. If this was
the style the army lived in –

'I was cooking for officers in France,' Niggler said, 'when all
we'd got was "K" rations. That's the time it finds you – when
you got to conjure up trout with almonds and duckling in red
wine sauce out of "K" rations.'

'Conjure is the word,' Mr Featherstone said.

A little later he looked up to see the Pearce attacking a
chicken bone, already deprived of most of its meat, with the
voracity of a starved dog, gnawing at it as she grasped it in both
hands. Monty was more polite; she merely sucked at hers, as at
a lollipop.

Niggler was shovelling in green peas with a knife and explaining between swigs of beer, how he had once had a delightful little arrangement with a countess at a château. Very
convenient – sort of give and take –

'She gave and you took, I suppose,' Mr Featherstone said.

Niggler made noises indicating that his pride was hurt.

'No: I gave and *she* took,' he said. 'She had some of the best
brandy you ever tasted.'

Niggler's astute mention of brandy reminded the Pearce

that she had been saving half a bottle since Christmas. About this time Niggler asked permission to take off his jacket and sat for the rest of the time in his braces, occasionally belching. Now and then he described incidents of a romantic order involving girls in Flemish farmhouses, to which Monty and the Pearce listened with a combination of laughter, envy, and awe.

Soon the brandy appeared, together with a cigar for Niggler and one for the Pearce. The evening darkened and cuckoos ceased to call. With fluting charm Monty asked what time the lorry would be leaving in the morning. Whatever time it was there would be an early cup of tea.

At the same time the Pearce reminded Niggler of the weekly flutter. She was going to have three pounds on this week; the meal had been so good she felt positively reckless. Monty said she would stick to her usual two – she had been reading her stars that morning and they pronounced in favour of some caution in financial affairs.

'Better give you the money now,' the Pearce said, 'in case it slips our minds tomorrow,' and Niggler pocketed the fiver with the polite and slightly absent restraint of a man accepting a cigarette.

Having pocketed the money, disposed of most of the brandy and finished the cigar Niggler announced that he was just about ready to kip down. Mr Featherstone was going to have a real bed in the spare room but he, Niggler, would be perfectly happy on the kitchen sofa. He'd kipped there before.

With something like choral adoration in their voices the two ladies said 'Good night' and thanked Niggler over and over again for his company, his generosity and above all his thoughtfulness. It was so thoughtful of him to remember the chickens; it had absolutely made their day.

Left alone in the kitchen, Niggler prepared to kip down. He had scarcely begun to remove his collar and tie when a tap on the kitchen door was followed by Monty's whispered voice asking if she might come in.

'It was about the chickens,' she said.

As she attempted to slip a pound note into his hand Niggler made a pretence of recoiling painfully, as if the money would positively burn holes in his fingers.

'No, no, no,' he said. He spoke as if being mildly insulted. 'Couldn't do that. They were a present from me.'

'Please,' she said. 'Please. Not another word. I knew the Pearce wouldn't do it because she's so frightfully forgetful. And I couldn't very well do it in front of Mr Featherstone because it would have been embarrassing.'

Niggler, accepting this further largesse with something like a sigh, presently started to take off his shoes and trousers. He was still unlacing his shoes when the Pearce announced her presence by giving a sharp masculine 'Rum-tiddly-um-pum' on the kitchen door. She too had come about the chickens.

With a voice wrung by injured pride Niggler protested that he couldn't accept a penny for the chickens. It was all done in the name of friendship.

'Of course. I know that,' the Pearce said. 'But even so you have to pay your friend. Don't be foolish, dear boy. Take it – I might have forgotten it. You don't know how forgetful I am.'

With a heavy show of reluctance Niggler pocketed another pound.

'Soon,' he said, as if in an attempt to atone for it all, 'the green peas'll be in. When they are I'll try to get a couple o' nice young ducks. I think I know where I could pick up some good 'uns.'

'Delicious, delicious,' she said. 'Good night, dear boy. Sweet dreams. We'll call you at six with tea.'


'They're the sort what don't get married,' Niggler said to Mr Featherstone as they drove away the following morning, the information being imparted as if it were a profound discovery.

After a good breakfast of bacon, sausage, and eggs, with plenty of toast, marmalade, and coffee, Niggler was also well provisioned for the day with two bottles of beer, several hard-boiled eggs, a hand of bananas, a stout wedge of fruit cake, and half a cold chicken still plentifully packed with stuffing.

'Speaking of marriage,' Mr Featherstone said, 'are you married?'

'Oh! yes,' Niggler said. 'Don't see much of the old trouble-and-strife, though.'

'Yes, I suppose it's rather hard sometimes.'

'Question of give and take,' Niggler said. 'Can't have it all ways, can you? I mean if you're here you can't be there, can you?'

Mr Featherstone waited for some moments for this enigmatic sentence to be enlarged upon but after an almost sad if not sorrowful sigh from Niggler the dark hints went wholly unpursued.

It was a fresh, sunny morning, with cuckoos calling everywhere, and there was a spring sweetness in the air so far unblemished by Niggler's clouds of shag.

'Lovely morning,' Niggler kept saying. 'Good to be alive.'

Mr Featherstone eventually remarked with restrained acidity that he should think it was too. After what happened last night.

'Here, steady on, Feather,' Niggler spoke again with an air of profoundly wounded pride. 'You're comin' the old philosophical a bit this morning, ain't you?'

'Philosophical! I've just decided what your philosophy is,' Mr Featherstone said. 'It's one of the oldest. What's yours is mine, what's mine's my own.'

'Here, that's a bit orf,' Niggler said, 'ain't it? That's a bit steep.'

'Look what you did to the ladies,' Mr Featherstone said. 'You know perfectly well you put less than half that money on the horses.'

'Yes, but they had the chickens. I gave 'em the chickens, didn't I?'

'But good God, man, they weren't yours to give! They belonged to that wretched farmer –'

'Yes, but I done him a good turn, didn't I?'

'Good turn?'

'I give him the number of that Ford Zephyr, didn't I?'

'But there wasn't any Ford Zephyr!'

'No,' Niggler said darkly, 'but there might have been. You never know. Probably full of blokes on the fiddle too.'

'For Heaven's sake, man,' Mr Featherstone said, 'how do you know they'd be on the fiddle even if they were there?'

'Everybody's on the fiddle,' Niggler said blandly. 'You included.'

'Me?'

'Course. You're fiddlin' lifts. You're a college man. You ought to be bleedin' well payin' good money to the railways, but you're hitchin' lifts instead. No wonder the railways don't make no bleedin' profits. How the bleedin' hell can they with blokes like you fiddlin' and mugs like me harbourin' you in it all the time?'

Delivered with steady but good-natured passion, this speech had the effect of reducing Mr Featherstone to complete silence for some time.

'That's me,' Niggler said. 'Joe Mug. Always doin' everybody a good turn. Gettin' chickens here. Geese there. Cookin' 'em. Layin' money on the gee-gees. Givin' lifts. Blimey, I've saved you the bleedin' fare to Penzance, ain't I?'

Mr Featherstone was beginning to think that this was, perhaps, a prudent moment in which to change the subject.

'I must say too that I thought that beer-trap for rats was a bit tall.'

With a voice of mild innocence Niggler confessed that in fact it was, in a way.

'How do you mean, in a way?'

'Well,' Niggler said, 'they was overrun with rats and asked me if I knew of anything that could be done. All they had to drink in the house at that time was milk and water. I couldn't go rat-catchin' on that. I'd had eight hours drivin' in heavy rain. So I said I'd set my patent beer-trap if they'd get the beer in. They did.'

Mr Featherstone laughed briefly.

'You'll be telling me next you've got a patent brandy-trap for pheasants.'

Niggler answered by saying that as a matter of fact he had. You soaked raisins in brandy – or gin, or whisky, it didn't much matter – and stuck them on fish-hooks. The pheasants went for them bald-headed and dropped down like flies.

Again Mr Featherstone deemed it a prudent moment in which to change the subject.

'By the way, speaking of driving,' he said, 'shall we make Penzance tonight?'

'Not tonight,' Niggler said. 'Have to kip down with some more friends of mine.'

'Ladies again?'

'Wimmin again,' Niggler said. 'Mother and daughter. Very nice. Daughter about your age. Might suit you.'

With caustic brevity Mr Featherstone made it clear that he hardly cared for such casual associations.

'That may be,' Niggler said. He had started to roll, with customary deftness, one of his lethal cigarettes. 'But when you're like me, away from home an' all that, you've got to look arter these little kips. They save lolly. They come in handy.'

Smoke filled the air in pungent, evil clouds.

'You ain't in all that much of a tearin' hurry, are you?' Niggler said. 'I mean is Auntie expectin' you?'

'Oh! no, oh! no. I was merely asking.'

'That's all right, then. Didn't want to keep Auntie waitin'.'

'Oh! she simply expects me when she sees me. She never worries. She's got her companion and all the servants around. Plenty to occupy her.'

'All the servants? Difficult to get these days, ain't they?'

'Oh! They've all been with her for donkey's years.'

Fag dangling precariously from one side of his mouth, Niggler remarked out of the other that it sounded as if Auntie was pretty well breeched. 'You know, comfortable?'

'Oh! yes, you could say that. She has this really rather nice house by the sea.'

'Goin' to spend all your holiday with her?'

'I always do. You see, it's really my home. I've got no father or mother. She's my guardian and all that.'

After listening to all this Niggler stubbed out his fag and remarked that it seemed funny that Auntie didn't send him the railway fare.

'Oh! she would. Like a shot. But it's more fun this way.'

'I see. I just thought she might be on the near side or summat like that.'

On the contrary, Mr Featherstone confided. She was most generous, without being extravagantly so. She always saw him very comfortable at the beginning of every term.

It now seemed an excellent moment, Niggler thought, for him to change the subject.

'This friend of mine and her daughter keep a very nice pull-up dinin'-rooms,' he said. 'The grub's not bad. They often have very nice mackerel done with mustard in the season. And about the best sausage-and-mash in the country. Don't know if you like that?'

Oddly enough, Mr Featherstone said, it was one of his favourite dishes. There was a place in Oxford to which he often went and they did it pretty superbly there.

'Then you'll be quids-in tonight,' Niggler said. 'Don't suppose it'll cost us a penny either.'

'No? You seem to have very generous friends on all sides.'

'Well –'

Niggler, pausing, seemed to drift away into a sudden dream. The face that in its many distortions seemed to have been flattened by a mighty blow softened appreciably, in a not in-sensitive way, almost in fact sentimental. The darting blue eyes seemed to reach out and, as it were, finger that distant landscape of leafing hawthorns, budding oaks and occasional cowslip fields with a warm, fond sense of anticipation.

'Well, it's a bit difficult to explain,' Niggler said. 'It's a bit more than friendship with Lil an' me. Well, I mean, we got a sort of special arrangement.'

The very nice pull-up dining-rooms, called The Rose of Killarney Café, consisted of a stucco bungalow and two disused railway carriages painted bright vermilion with window frames in equally brilliant mustard. Two tin chimneys, looking very like leg pieces from a suit of armour, stuck out of the carriage tops, belching dark smoke across a hillside already cloudy with impending rain.

An odour as if perhaps cart grease were being fried came out of the railway carriages, the windows of which were thickly steamed with fog. Across the cinder pull-in outside the café a few lorries were parked but not half so many, Niggler said, as usual. It was Friday night and blokes were making for home.

Inside the dining-rooms the odour of frying cart grease not only became increasingly more powerful. It was now shot with searching flavours as diverse as fish and bacon, pickles and mutton chops, sausages, boiling ham and vinegar.

A big fat girl of seventeen or eighteen with hands of dough and a home-style perm was serving at red-topped tables where several drivers sat washing down plates of food, mostly sausage-and-mash, with large pots of steaming tea. The permed hair, very blonde, had something of the violent appearance of a yellow golliwog recently frightened by something very shocking in the dark.

'Oh! Mum, it's Niggler! Mum, Niggler's here!'

The voice of the girl was plummy. It fell on Mr Featherstone's ears with all the distastefulness of a moist and disconcerting kiss.

'Be back in a jiff, Feather,' Niggler said. 'Must pop into the kitchen. Make yourself at home. How's Eadie?' he asked of the fat girl. 'This is my friend, Mr Feather. Expect he'd like a cuppa.'

'Any relation of Mrs Feather?' the fat girl said and laughed in Mr Featherstone's face with rich and companionable fervour from a chest ample as a pumpkin. 'Don't suppose so?'

'My name,' he said, 'is Featherstone.'

Meanwhile, in the kitchen, Niggler was being not only cordially but desperately embraced by a stoutish woman who had previously been frying sausages and was now in an almost fainting attitude.

'Oh! Niggler, Niggler. Thought you were never going to turn up.'

Niggler's acceptance of the fourth of a chain of impulsively damp kisses seemed to be less passionate than philosophical.

'Couldn't do it, Lil. Had to go up north last week. Right up to Doncaster.'

Lil released what appeared to be the beginnings of a sob, either of relief or joy, and Niggler responded by giving her the comfort of a tender hand consolingly placed midway across her bosom.

'Oh! not now. Not yet,' she said. 'You'll have me all worked up –'

With quivering reluctance Lil removed the hand and turned back to the frying of sausages, of which there were two dozen or more spluttering and popping in a large black pan.

In an undistinguished sort of way Lil was handsome. A bonnet of fluffy permed brown hair sat above a face that was creamy in colour and smooth as alabaster. The large coffee-dark eyes and the biggish soft lips were emotional, fervent and never still.

'Oh! Niggler, I'm dying to ask – did you get it?'

Niggler adopted an attitude of light mystification and surprise, as if utterly unable to follow what Lil was on about.

'It?'

With what seemed to be the beginnings of another, deeper sob Lil abandoned the sausages and reminded Niggler with incautious fervour that she was talking about the ring – the engagement ring.

'You said you'd bring it this time. You promised faithful.'

Airily Niggler confessed he had but at the same time, he told her, he'd been very, very short for the past two weeks. It was bad. One or two dead certs had let him down.

'I'm still a tenner short,' he said, 'for the right ring. The one I want.'

'You could always get it on the never-never, couldn't you?'

'Not this one. I'm getting this one from a pal. He's in that trade.' A wide disarming smile brought his features into sudden flower, so that Lil felt herself melting. 'Diamond and rubies set in platinum – it ain't half a beaut.'

'Oh! Niggler dearie, Niggler.'

'It's going to be a big bargain too – two hundred pound ring and he's letting me have it for fifty.'

With almost tearful joy, brown eyes moistly dancing, Lil confessed that she couldn't believe her ears. Was he sure there wasn't something funny about it? It hadn't been nicked or anything, had it, the ring? They didn't want any funny business.

'I ask no questions,' Niggler said, with a passing suggestion of dignity, almost as if affronted. 'I ask no questions.'

'It sounds an awful difference to me. Two hundred and –'

'All I know,' Niggler said, 'he's in that trade.'

'But will he hold it for you? How soon can you get it do you suppose?'

'He'll hold it till I get back from this trip,' Niggler said. 'Arter that –'

A threatening despair seized Lil's ample body and made it go taut. She didn't want to lose that ring, she started saying, she'd give her head rather than lose that ring.

'Listen, Niggler dearie, I tell you what. How if I lend you the other tenner? Long as you pay it back soon –'

Not on her nelly, Niggler told her, again with dignified calm. He didn't do that sort of thing.

'I'd be glad to. Honest, I'd be glad to. After all it isn't as if we're strangers exactly –'

Impulsively she seized his face and kissed him again, an action that seemed merely to have the effect of stiffening Niggler into firmer, more honest resolve.

No use her talking. No use her keeping on about it. His mind was made up. He'd get the ring somehow.

'I know how you feel, dearie,' Lil said, 'but you've only got to say. Shall we talk about it tonight?'

'Eadie's coming,' Niggler said.

Into the kitchen bounced Eadie, eager and kittenish in spite of her size. Two customers were cribbing about the sausages being so long, she told her mother.

'Just coming up,' Lil said. 'Had a lot to do.'

'I don't think your friend Mr Feather's feeling very well,' Eadie said. 'He says he's feeling the cold.'

'A plate of hot sausage'll soon put him right,' Lil said. 'All right for you too, Niggler? Sausages, eggs and mash?'

Niggler, giving Lil a departing friendly squeeze in the back that seemed momentarily to paralyse her into a dream, said it would suit him fine and then went back into the café to talk to Mr Featherstone.

'Hurry up, Mum,' Eadie said. 'Don't just stand there. They'll start cribbing again.'

'Let 'em crib,' Lil said. 'Niggler's going to buy me a two hundred and fifty pound ring.' New ecstasies began to dart through her at the mere thought of it. 'Diamonds and rubies in platinum –'

Back in the café Mr Featherstone was beginning to feel that he couldn't stand the odour of frying cart grease much longer. He was feeling dispirited, tired, and sick. In a depressed voice he confessed to Niggler that he thought he'd caught a chill in the cab. It was all across his back and he could feel a tonsil coming up. Would it be all the same to everyone if he had a glass of hot milk and went to bed?

'Have some hot sausage,' Niggler said.

Mr Featherstone came within a fraction of being sick. From across the café came a strange sucking sound and he turned to see a big ox of a man, crouched over a table, drinking tea from a saucer. A paralysis far more formidable than Lil's seized him a moment later, so that he could neither speak nor move, and it was as if from foggy distances that he heard Niggler say:

'Expect it'll be all right. Eadie'll see to it. I'll ask Eadie.'

Five minutes later he was tucked up in the bungalow, in a black iron bed, with an old patch-work quilt on top of him. The patch-work quilt had already induced in him the feeling that he was in the centre of some crazy, light-headed dream when Eadie boomed in, fresh and brisk as a fledgeling, with a bottle of aspirin and a mug of hot milk on a tray.

'Here you are, dear. I put a drop of whisky in the milk. That ought to do the trick.'

She set the tray on a bedside table and then sat down sloppily, with a big bump, on the bed. Mr Featherstone's head started rocking with deep reverberations, but Eadie merely laughed boisterously and as it seemed without purpose at something and then said:

'You're lucky to travel with Niggler. He's nice. He's a lovely man. Mum's going to marry him soon.'

'Great God,' Mr Featherstone said.

It was a dream, it was immoral, he started telling himself. It couldn't go on.

'They're going to get engaged. It's been a sort of whirlwind courtship.'

'Whirlwind?'

In a voice that hardly belonged to him Mr Featherstone whispered the one word and then said he'd rather supposed that her mother was married already.

'Oh! no,' Eadie said. 'Oh! no,' but offered no further explanation.

Mr Featherstone said in an unconvincing fashion, now gently sipping hot milk, that he had sort of formed the impression that Niggler was married too.

'Oh! no,' she said, 'how could he be? He's going to buy mum a two hundred and fifty pound ring. Diamonds and rubies in platinum.'

Mr Featherstone, his head rocking, was silent. It was a subject he felt too tired and too dispirited to pursue any further and soon he was drifting off into inchoate dreams, madly struggling with truth and fantasy and the crazy patterns of the quilt on the bed.

It was much later, past eleven o'clock, when Niggler sat in the kitchen with Lil on his knee. Ecstasy in her had never diminished all evening. It had kept her eyes continually dancing and now, in a throaty whisper and with a long incontinent squeeze of Niggler's body, she asked if he thought it wasn't time they went to bed?

'Got something to say first,' Niggler said, solemn in every feature.

'Oh?'

'I told you a bit of a lie this afternoon.'

'Not about the ring?' she said. 'You don't mean you can't get it?'

'It's about the ring, but not that.'

'What then?'

'It ain't a tenner I'm short of,' he said. 'It's twenty.'

Suddenly almost as kittenish as Eadie, Lil burst into fresh peals of relieved, ecstatic laughter.

'Only that!' she said. 'You had me scared for a moment, you really did.' She started to give him another chain of damp impulsive kisses. 'You mean you're actually going to let me lend you the money?'

'I'll have to,' Niggler said, almost as if depressed with sadness at the thought of his own shortcomings. 'I don't want to let you down, Lil, and it's the only way I can think of.'

Still dopey under the effect of aspirin, a swollen tonsil and the notion that he had been wrestling with a strange nightmare Mr Featherstone sat in the cab next morning dumbly staring at the unfolding countryside.

Niggler, blowing shag, didn't appear to be very talkative either and it was some miles farther on before he said:

'You're a bit quiet this morning. Feather. Not very philosophical? Don't feel too good?'

'Not too bad, thanks,' Mr Featherstone said. 'Actually I was thinking about something I heard yesterday.'

'Oh?'

'Eadie told me,' Mr Featherstone said, 'that you were pro-posing to get engaged to her mother. It can't be true?'

'That's right,' Niggler said. 'I am.'

'But good God, man, you're married already!'

'I know,' Niggler said.

'But great Heavens, you can't do it. It's called bigamy – haven't you heard? It's one of the things they put you inside for!'

'Oh! I ain't going to marry her,' Niggler said. 'Just going to get engaged. That's all.'

'But good God, man, why?'

'She wants me to,' Niggler said. 'She's set her heart on it.'

'Good grief, I daresay she has, but – '

Mr Featherstone struggled dopily to pull himself together. His head was bumping wildly again. It was probably the aspirin, he kept thinking. He'd taken too much aspirin. Aspirin and whisky together.

'You must be out of your mind,' he told Niggler. 'What's this crazy idea about a two hundred and fifty pound ring?'

Niggler laughed, as it seemed despairingly.

'That's a fairy-tale,' he said. 'Eadie must have made that one up. Me? How could I get that kind of money?'

'How could you think of it at all?' Mr Featherstone said. 'Besides, isn't she married? What about Eadie?'

'Well, she is in a way.'

'What do you mean,' Mr Featherstone almost shouted, 'in a way?'

'Her husband left her eight or nine years ago,' Niggler said. 'They say that lets her free.'

'Free,' Mr Featherstone said, 'I love this word free. You'll be telling me next you're free.'

'No. I got to get that ring though. I got to borrow the money somehow. If I don't – '

'Well, what?'

'She'll throw herself in the river. I was up all night with her, trying to console her. Couldn't pacify her nohow. She was in a terrible track because I hadn't brought the ring. I promised I would, see? Made a solemn promise. She'll throw herself in the river. I know.'

'But you can't do it, man. It's immoral.'

At these remarks Niggler looked really hurt, almost dejected.

'Don't be hard, Feather. I got to get that ring afore I get back to the Rose of Killarney again. Else I'll never sleep no more.'

'But for God's sake why?'

'I want to do her a good turn,' Niggler said. 'I want to make her happy.'

Speechless, Mr Featherstone sat plunged in deflated silence while Niggler, with hands that seemed touchingly uncertain now, rolled another fag.

'Didn't you hear her cryin'?' he inquired in unsteady tones of Mr Featherstone. 'She cried all night. I can hear her now.'

Mr Featherstone confessed that, drugged as he was with aspirin, he hadn't heard a sound.

'Heart-renderin',' Niggler said. 'I got to get that ring. I got to borrow a fiver somehow today.'

Mr Featherstone begged Niggler not to look at *him*. He was down to his last ten bob.

'I wouldn't dream of askin' *you*,' Niggler said. 'Wouldn't do that. Only I wondered – '

'Yes?'

'Would Auntie help? Couldn't you get it from Auntie? It's only till tomorrow.'

'Tomorrow? Why tomorrow?'

'I get paid at the depot here tomorrow,' Niggler said. 'I could easy drop the fiver into your auntie's house on my way back.'

'But couldn't you get the ring after you get paid?'

'No. I won't have time. But I will have time this afternoon. We'll be there by three o'clock.'

Mr Featherstone sat silent, either as if cogitating or unwilling or even both.

'I hoped you'd say yes. I hoped you'd help me out,' Niggler said in tones of such sad reproach that Mr Featherstone's conscience instantly started biting him. 'After all I done you a good turn. Two free kips, two free dinners and a long ride.'

Depressedly Mr Featherstone agreed that that was true. Two free kips, two free dinners and a long ride. Not to speak of the chickens.

'After all,' Niggler said. 'It's only for a day, Feather. I'm only doing it to make her happy. I only want to make her happy.'

It would not have surprised Mr Featherstone at this moment if Niggler had wept on his shoulder and suddenly, in tones almost consolatory, he said:

'All right, Niggler, forget it now. I'll do what I can. I promise I'll do what I can. She isn't a bad soul at all, Auntie.'

Two hours later Niggler was leaning out of the cab of the lorry, which was parked outside a largish red-brick Edwardian house against the porch of which a large white magnolia was in full blossom in the April sun.

'Well, ta very much again, Feather,' he said. 'I'll be droppin' by tomorrow. It'll be pretty early – I'll slip the envelope through the door. So long.'

'So long, Niggler,' Mr Featherstone said. 'So long.'

Niggler started to let in the clutch. It was a beautiful day: good to be alive. Soon it would be summer, the time of green peas and new potatoes, nice young ducklings and apple sauce. He must be watching out for some nice young ducklings soon. The really good time, with the flat season in full swing and the Derby and all that, was just coming. In fact it was here.

'Well, so long, Feather,' Niggler said. He leaned from the cab with a grin as broad as a barrel, shaking a still dopey and sniffing Mr Featherstone with splendid warmth and gratitude by the hand. 'Shan't forget. Best of luck with the old philosophical.'

Finally, as the lorry moved away, he gave one of those spontaneous croaky laughs that were so remarkably like the noise made by a strangled chicken.

'See you on the Christmas-tree.'

# The World is Too Much With Us

'Good girl, Georgina, nice girl,' Mr Plomley said. 'Another lovely big brown one.' Mr Plomley fondly held the large un-blemished egg in the palm of his hand, where it felt as smooth as a baby's cheek and warm as new-baked bread. 'An absolute beauty, dear.'

Georgina, the Rhode Island Red, always roosted in the old harmonium. That, Mr Plomley was sure, was what made her lay so well. It was a very comfortable and refined place for a hen like Georgina to roost in – he would have none of your precarious perches in old draughty roosts, where rats roved, for a hen like her. The curtains of the front parlour windows were of thick chenille, in a warm strawberry-jam shade, and Mr Plomley always kept them drawn until nine o'clock, so that Georgina could sleep late if she wanted to. There was no rough rousing of Georgina at the crack of dawn, like any common hen.

'I've brought your mash, dear. Warm this morning. Now September's started you can just feel that chill in the air.'

Mr Plomley, who still showed some evidence of having once been dapper, was now rather stout, absent-eyed and shabby. His face was an amiable pink melon with misty sepia eyes and his hands as he drew the curtains and placed the white china bowl of faintly steaming mash on the top of the harmonium were like stale and podgy sausages.

'Sleep well, dear? I hope they didn't disturb you across the road? I mean the new people in the shop. They seemed to be hammering away for hours.'

Mr Plomley kissed Georgina lightly on the comb and she in

turn seemed to return the compliment by an oblique stroke of her beak across his rather untidy moustache, with its slightly gingery curls.

'Eat up, dear, while it's warm.' Mr Plomley put a hand under Georgina and gently raised her up until she stood over the mash-bowl. She proceeded to eat rather daintily, eyes slightly baggy, and Mr Plomley said: 'What do you think? I've got something to tell you. That's your one hundred and forty-ninth egg this year. Aren't you the proud girl? One more and it'll be a hundred and fifty.'

With slow and affectionate fingers Mr Plomley stroked Georgina all the way down her smooth brown back. The warm touch of her feathers gave him a curiously exhilarated sensation like that of touching naked flesh. With a blissful croak or two Georgina seemed to acknowledge this while still eating and Mr Plomley said:

'Won't be a minute, dear. Be back in a minute. No hurry. Just take your time.'

When Mr Plomley came back from the kitchen a few minutes later, carrying a baby's hair-brush, a sponge, a box of dusting-powder, a pair of scissors and a bowl of soapy water, he was chuckling to himself aloud.

'Whatever you'll say to me I don't know,' he said. 'Simply can't think.' Mr Plomley, in the course of logging Georgina's one hundred and forty-ninth egg in the marbled-covered ledger he had long kept for the purpose, had suddenly felt himself obliged to do some speedy revision in arithmetic. 'At first I thought I must have added it up all wrong. I suppose I was excited. But no – it's absolutely all right, dear. An accountant would certify it – it *is* your hundred and fiftieth, Georgina, it really is!'

If there seemed to be a certain contentment arising from self-satisfaction in Georgina's drooping eye, almost a smugness, Mr Plomley failed to notice it. Instead he embraced Georgina about the neck with both hands, pressing her against his chest as another man might have pressed a girl.

'Now you've really got to be made a nice, clean, pretty girl, haven't you? We've really got to doll up today, haven't we? And what about something special – eh, for lunch? Some of those nice coffee-beans? And a toothful of whisky?'

Over the years Georgina had developed a decided taste in coffee-beans – they were perhaps the reason, Mr Plomley thought, for the rich and perfect brownness of the eggs – and he in turn, as he took a whisky or two or perhaps even three or four with his lunch, had induced in her a taste for something stronger. Neither of them got exactly drunk at midday but most afternoons they were very comatose and sleepy and often they ended up with a long snooze together.

'I rather think I'm out of coffee-beans. I'll have to pop across to the shop. Heaven knows what the new people are like – haven't set eyes on them yet.'

In the course of the next few minutes Mr Plomley proceeded to wash Georgina's legs and comb in soapy water, carefully trim her claws with the scissors and clean and brush her feathers with the powder and the baby brush.

'And a very pretty girl, too, aren't we? A very, very pretty girl. Boy's very proud of you.'

On very special occasions, such as this one, Mr Plomley referred to himself as 'boy'. The word served to bring a new intimacy into their relationship and sometimes, in consequence, his voice seemed almost to curdle with pleasure.

'Boy won't be long now. Just popping across to the shop. Like to get down and stretch your legs?' He lifted Georgina off the harmonium with the palm of one hand and let her flap to the parlour floor. 'And what about something else a little special? Ice-cream?' Georgina had also developed a taste in ice-cream, especially the sort that is frozen in fruit flavours on sticks. 'Lemon or raspberry? I'll see what they have.'

Presently Mr Plomley slipped on a beige alpaca jacket and walked through the garden towards the road, occasionally brushing his moustache with his finger tips and muttering absently to himself in disjoined words. The morning was

pleasantly brilliant for early September. The summer had
been mostly dry and warm and already from the pine-trees that
screened the boundaries of the garden large sere brown cones
were falling. Not only did the pines shut out all view of the
big red-brick house from the road; Mr Plomley had also made
sure that no one if possible ever came near it by studding the
cement top of the garden wall with broken bottles and a battle
front of thick barbed wire. He had also fixed to the heavy gate
a large metal notice which read:

|     | HAWKERS |
|-----|---------|
|     | CIRCULARS |
| NO  | SALESMEN |
|     | TRADESMEN |
|     | TRAMPS |

ALL COMMUNICATIONS TO BE LEFT HERE

By contrast the shop across the road, with a garden so small
that the solitary laburnum tree shading its ten square yards of
grass seemed overpowering, looked accessible and friendly, as
village shops so often do.

'Good morning, sir. Nice bright morning. Does your heart
good to be alive, eh?'

Across the shop counter, on which stood what he knew to
be a gleaming new bacon-slicer, Mr Plomley found himself
facing, with surprise, a well-built, comfortably breasted
woman of fifty or so wearing an emerald overall, turquoise
ear-rings and a massive crop of orange hair. The burning nature
of the hair so startled him that it was some moments before he
could say, uneasily and absently:

'Good morning. Yes, I suppose it's a sort of Indian summer,
isn't it?'

'I love this country air. Never thought I should, but it gets
you.'

Still uneasy, Mr Plomley tried hard to take his gaze away
from the inflammable pile behind the bacon-slicer. At the same

time it occurred to him that he ought to introduce himself and
he said:

'Oh! I'm Plomley – from The Pines, across the way. I
always had a monthly account when Mrs Hardstaff was here.
I use the shop a lot. I hope that's all right with you?'

The orange hair, almost tribally rich and brilliant, seemed to
rock from side to side as the woman in the emerald overall
twice patted it from the back with a generous hand.

'Oh! anything's all right with me. Must keep the customers
happy.'

She laughed heavily and moistly. The muscles of her throat
rippled like those of a large cat. This fleshy rippling so dis-
quieted Mr Plomley that he said:

'It was awfully sad about Mrs Hardstaff. Going off so
suddenly. I see you still haven't changed the name over the shop.'

'Going to be done tomorrow.' She laughed again. 'Not
sure what to put up though yet. Can't decide if it's to be plain
Phoebe Spencer or the Nice'n Cozy Stores. What do you
think?'

Mr Plomley, after some hesitation, said he thought that undoubtedly plain Phoebe Spencer sounded the more dignified.

'Oh! I don't care about dignity. I want something bright.
Got to get the customers in somehow. If they won't come
willing hit them over the head with a hammer. That's what
Joe used to say.'

'Joe?'

'My husband. He got run down by a train last year, working outside Paddington. That's why – '

Before she could finish her sentence a sudden wailing whistle
shot out with ferocious impact from somewhere behind the
shop.

'That's my kettle. Won't be a jiff. Just going to make myself
a cuppa tea. Have one with me, will you?'

Mr Plomley had no time to frame any sort of reply before
she disappeared through the door behind the counter. The
piercing whistle stopped as suddenly as it had begun. A

moment or two later she was back behind the counter, saying:

'Didn't hear you say if you'd have a 'cuppa or not. No trouble. I'm dying for one.'

'Well, really, no. I don't think so. Thank you very much all the same.'

'That's all right. Well, what can I do for you?'

'Well, coffee-beans for one thing. I think two pounds –'

'Oh! you prefer coffee. I see.'

'No, no. Not really. They're for Georgina.'

Phoebe Spencer's eyes, which were sugary and greenish, like large lumps of candied peel, roved slowly from Mr Plomley to the shelves behind and above her head.

'Think you've got me there. In fact I know you have. Haven't really got sorted out yet. The carpenters didn't leave till late last night. But I can ring up my wholesalers and get some over by lunch-time.'

Mr Plomley said it was rather disappointing about the coffee but so long as it arrived some time during the day it didn't really matter. He'd promised Georgina, that was all.

'Oh! it'll be over. Slit my throat. Anything else, mean-time?'

'I think two lemon splits and a tin of baby powder. If you haven't got lemon ones raspberry will do. Oh! yes and three packets of pop-corn.'

'Nothing like keeping the kids happy,' Phoebe Spencer said. 'How many you got?'

With shyness Mr Plomley confessed that there were no kids. It was all for Georgina.

'Oh! your wife, I see.'

This time Mr Plomley was too shy both to confess that he had no wife and that Georgina was, in fact, a hen. It had always seemed to him something very nearly approaching sacrilege to disclose Georgina, except by name, to the world at large. He could not bear that her existence might be misunderstood or, worse still, become an affair of ridicule. Consequently they kept themselves very much to themselves.

'Well, no, we're just friends. We sort of – well, you know – get along together.'

Phoebe Spencer's large candied-peel eyes expanded with abrupt and almost lilting surprise. The things that went on in the country! She seemed about to give a juicy sort of whistle. Her fleshy lips actually pursed themselves together for the act and then suddenly opened in a smile of total understanding.

'Bet you have a tiff or two though, sometimes, eh?' With fresh embarrassment Mr Plomley could have sworn that Phoebe Spencer winked at him. 'Nice to make up though, I always say.'

'I don't think Georgina and I have ever had a cross word,' Mr Plomley said.

'No? That's nice. Well, there's the two splits. Both lemon. And the baby powder.' The baby powder was a bit odd, she thought, wasn't it? She couldn't quite fathom the baby powder. 'And the three bags of pop-corn. That all for now?'

'There was something else at the back of my mind.'

'Matches? Cigarettes? Baked beans? Butter? All right for butter? Gone down again.'

Mr Plomley was about to say that he was all right for butter when he remembered, with a vexed exclamation, what it was he wanted.

'Of course. It's one of those small pen-fillers I want. Mrs Hardstaff got a couple of dozen in specially for me. Georgina's always breaking them. She's inclined to nip the end off when she's having her whisky.'

'Oh! does she?'

The inquisitive nature of Phoebe Spencer's stare died this time from sheer astonishment. The big peel-like eyes were merely blank with defeat.

'I suppose she could have it in some other way,' Mr Plomley said, 'but that's the way she's always had it. Habit, I suppose.'

'Sounds a bit difficult, your girl friend, if you don't mind me saying so.'

'Oh! no, Georgina isn't difficult. Oh! no, she's easy. She's a frightfully clever little thing too. And terribly affectionate. Nobody in the world could be more affectionate.'

The candour of these disclosures left Phoebe Spencer so bewildered that she had to add up the cost of the splits, the pop-corn, the baby powder and the pen-filler three times and was even then not sure she had the total right.

'Seven and ninepence. I think. Well, call it that anyway. Not sure about the pen-filler, that's all.'

'Mrs Hardstaff always charged a shilling.' Absently Mr Plomley took a pound note from his pocket and put it on the counter and said, while waiting for his change: 'You won't forget about the coffee? You'll get plenty of coffee in, won't you? Georgina more or less lives on coffee.'

Phoebe Spencer said yes, she'd remember the coffee and a moment later leaned across the counter to give Mr Plomley his change. Her deep breasts pressed forward roundly against the neck of the emerald overall. The pillar of orange hair seemed too to press forward and Mr Plomley felt himself instinctively re-coiling from a figure altogether too near, too real, too female and too handsome in its own oppressive fleshy way.

'Twelve and threepence change. Oh! Good God, what a fool I am. I clean forgot – you want it on the slate, don't you?'

'I completely forgot too,' Mr Plomley said. The nearness of the flesh was all of a sudden too much for him; the warm odour of Phoebe Spencer actually permeated the air. His thoughts rushed away towards Georgina and as he grabbed up his change he said: 'I'll take the change anyway. I'm rather short. I must get back to Georgina now. She likes her walk about this time.'

He fled towards the door in undisguised and fretful haste. The crackle of the pop-corn bags might have been the sound of splintered nerves.

'I'll ring for the coffee straight away,' she called after him. 'I'll bring it over directly it comes.'

'No, no, please. That's quite unnecessary. I can fetch it.'

Mr Plomley dived under the laburnum exactly as if ducking a shower of hostile poison arrows.

'It's early closing day,' he heard her call with eager throatiness. 'It's no trouble at all.'

After Mr Plomley had taken Georgina for her morning walk – he always walked quietly and gently behind her, letting her progress entirely at her own pace, simply keeping her from straying by occasional gentle touches of a hazel switch – they sat together for some time in the potting shed at the bottom of the garden, Mr Plomley on an old bag of peat, Georgina on his knee.

During all this time he felt a continuously strange and insidious disturbance about his encounter with Phoebe Spencer in the shop and now and then he felt a strong compulsion to tell Georgina all about it. The disturbance, he discovered, wasn't merely a physical one; it wasn't merely a matter of that vast tribal pyramid of orange hair, the large intrusive breasts, the fleshy voice and the eyes that were so like lumps of candied peel. He was worried that he hadn't been fair about Georgina. Out of an excessive shyness he had failed to be frank. Now Mrs Spencer clearly believed that Georgina was a girl and as a result he felt that he had, in a sense, let Georgina down.

'I'm terribly sorry about it, dear,' he told her several times. 'But I just don't want anybody intruding. That's the reason. We're perfectly all right as it is. We don't want people nosing around.'

It was precisely for these reasons that Mr Plomley liked to do all his own shopping; why no one ever came in to clean or cook or dig or tidy up the weeds. Mr Plomley and Georgina got on splendidly in isolation. It couldn't possibly have been better. Their lives were woven together like those of two figures in a piece of folk-lore: an eternal pattern of pure brown eggs, rewarding coffee-beans and ice-cream splits, communicative little walks and frequent tots of whisky.

'I just hope she won't come over with the coffee-beans, that's all,' he said. 'Anyway I could do with a drink. I expect you could too.'

Back in the front parlour Mr Plomley put Georgina on the top of the harmonium and uncorked a bottle of Johnny Walker. A certain nestling down of the feathers was Georgina's only answer to the sound of Mr Plomley pouring out the whisky. But she seemed to listen with a certain idle smugness as Mr Plomley filled the pen-filler with an inch or two of tea-coloured mixture and said:

'You've been such a good girl, dear. I didn't want anything like that to happen today. I felt so proud of you. That lovely egg. Anyway open up, dear. I made it just that tiny bit stronger today.'

After giving Georgina her first drink of the day through the pen-filler, Mr Plomley totted out a generous measure, more or less neat, for himself. As he took his first taste of it he turned to Georgina and, with an affectionate smile and pat on her comb, blessed her.

'I think I shall have an omelette for lunch,' he said, and then added quickly, as if in order not to hurt her feelings: 'Oh! not made with the new one. I wouldn't dream of that. And what about you?' Mr Plomley gave Georgina another affectionate pat on the comb. 'You know what I've got for you? Pop-corn and two lemon splits – a real special treat today.'

After two further whiskies, each rather more neat than before, Mr Plomley began to feel rather less anxious and distraught about Phoebe Spencer. She seemed to fade into a slightly golden haze, leaving himself and Georgina again in untroubled isolation.

By two o'clock he found that he cared very little whether his omelette was made of cheese or bacon or indeed if he ate it at all. The whisky had put a velvet cover on his appetite. He dropped into a big arm chair with Georgina on his knee, a half-empty glass in one hand and a lemon split in the other. Now and then Georgina, who had eaten up the three bags of pop-corn with voracious haste while the omelette was cooking, took torpid pecks at the glittering yellow cone.

Soon they were asleep together and it was not until Mr Plomley was in the middle of a dream in which Phoebe Spencer's whistling kettle was shrieking again that he woke with a start to realize that what he was really hearing was the front door-bell ringing loudly.

In a sleepy hurry he shut Georgina in the kitchen and went to answer the door, twice telling himself on the way that on no account, if it was Phoebe Spencer calling, would he let her in. But the door was no sooner open than she was swiftly across the threshold, pressing him backwards with the bag of coffee-beans.

'Mrs Spencer, no really you shouldn't – I could have come across –'

The uneasy realization that Phoebe Spencer was not merely dressed up but rather extravagantly so forced him into a hurried retreat in the direction of the sitting-room. The afternoon was warm. A strong scent of violets filled the air, wafted this way and that by Phoebe Spencer's every movement. The massive orange pyramid of hair seemed to blaze, thrown into flamboyant contrast by a low-necked dress of shimmering purple, smooth and tight as a banana skin on the curves of hips and bust and shoulders.

In a winning voice Phoebe Spencer said it was awfully nice of him to invite her in on such short acquaintance and Mr Plomley, who had done nothing of the kind, felt mortally afraid. A returning echo of his lunch-time whisky rose in his throat and stuck there with acid discomfort as Phoebe Spencer glanced searchingly about the room and said:

'Oh! you're all alone. I rather expected –'

'Georgina's out,' Mr Plomley said. 'Won't be back for a while.'

She seemed to take this as a signal to sit down and did so with friendly ease into the chair where Mr Plomley had fallen asleep with Georgina, the lemon split and the whisky.

The remains of the lemon split lay on the floor and Mr

Plomley hastily picked it up and stuck it on the mantelpiece. A lot of brown feathers lay about the floor too and Phoebe Spencer, who prided herself on being a person of sprucely clean and fastidious habits, noted them with vexed dismay. She didn't know about living in sin – let them get on with it if that's the way they wanted it – but a girl who could go out and leave the house looking like a hen run in the middle of the afternoon got no marks from her.

The house, wherever she turned to look, seemed an unholy sort of mess. Pop-corn bags lay torn to shreds in the hearth. Dirty plates and cutlery were piled on a chair and from the top of the harmonium there protruded a quaint straw-covered contraption, half hat, half basket, whose purposes defeated her. Nothing could have been further from her mind than that this was Georgina's roosting bag.

At this moment Mr Plomley detected with horror that his half-finished glass of whisky, over which he had fallen asleep, was still standing on the floor an inch or two from Phoebe Spencer's feet. Only by a miracle had she avoided kicking it over.

In his haste to pick it up he half-stumbled over the hearth-rug and found himself a moment later in a semi-kneeling position, facing the full view of Phoebe Spencer's rounded healthy knees unashamedly protruding from the fringe of the purple dress. He felt as embarrassed and nervous about this as if he had suddenly discovered her completely naked. A strange and discomforting sensation, utterly remote from anything he had ever experienced with Georgina, shot through him: a white-hot needle piercing all the central flabby marrow of his bones.

'It was just my whisky,' Mr Plomley explained. 'I dropped asleep and forgot it. Georgina and I generally have a couple at lunch-time.'

Untidy, not to say slovenly, but also a whisky drinker, Phoebe Spencer thought. There was nothing terribly serious about that, of course, but suddenly she found that there was building up, on the receptive canvas of her mind, a picture of a girl whose every quality was unlikeable. She was instinctively hostile to this picture; it irked her sharply. It would not have been by any means an exaggeration on her part to have said that she thought Georgina was a slut.

Paradoxically she immediately smiled on Mr Plomley, who was now putting the whisky glass on top of the dirty plates, and said:

'I must say I envy you. I mean having a companion and all that. You know, someone to talk to, to have near –'

Mr Plomley, still nervous from the unpremeditated vision of Phoebe Spencer's knees, said with sympathetic quietness that he supposed it must be very difficult, alone. He thought he understood how wretched it could be.

The softness of his voice might have been the brushing of a friendly hand. She held him for a few moments in warm and undisguised acceptance of his understanding, the large candied-peel eyes moistly aglow.

'You're a very sympathetic person,' she said, 'aren't you? I can feel it.'

Mr Plomley said he didn't know about that. It was merely –

'Oh! yes, you are. Georgina knows all about that, I'm sure.'

The deliberate introduction of Georgina into the conversation, prompted by a violent curiosity, merely succeeded in making Mr Plomley impossibly shy and nervous again. It had been on the tip of his tongue, once and for all, to explain Georgina away. It was better to be frank and avoid all misunderstanding.

Instead he merely smiled, without a word, and Phoebe Spencer took the smile to mean that she was right.

'I'm not sure I don't envy Georgina too,' she said and gave a short provoking laugh. 'Anyway I'll bet I've got good reason to.'

Mr Plomley said again that he wouldn't exactly say that. He didn't know what he would do without her, no doubt about that, but –

'You said she was pretty and clever.'

Oh! my God, Mr Plomley thought, I'm in an awful mess. He wished from the depths of his heart that people would leave him alone. He and Georgina, in isolation, understood each other. How on earth was it possible to explain a thing like that to a stranger? Desperately, knowing that every moment merely succeeded in making matters worse, he said:

'I really don't think you should attach too much importance to what I say about Georgina.'

The words were all that Phoebe Spencer needed to cheer, indeed encourage her.

'No?' she said. 'Well, if you say so. Perhaps I shall have the pleasure of meeting her some time?'

Mr Plomley said he doubted that. He confessed that Georgina was inclined to be rather difficult – Oh! no, not in the offensive sense he didn't mean. He simply meant that she kept herself an awful lot to herself. She was very much one on her own. In searching for some word adequately to describe Georgina's precious singularity he suddenly blurted out before he could stop himself:

'She broods.'

'Oh! does she?'

The words were dark; they hung in the air like raven's wings, poised with insinuation.

'Well, not quite in the sense that you think, I mean – '

Good God, Mr Plomley thought, what on earth am I talking about? A great shadow of self-accusation, darker even than Phoebe Spencer's words, shot through him. He was in an awful mess, a ghastly, irremediable, insoluble mess. He was really down the drain.

As if to rescue him from the dark recesses of his predicament Phoebe Spencer suddenly turned on him the full glow of her big candied-peel eyes and said:

'Joe used to be like that. Mostly when he was on night-shift. It was difficult to adapt himself – you know how I mean.'

Mr Plomley, desperately silent, had not the faintest idea at all what she could mean. He felt he would have liked another good strong whisky to pull himself together and he was actually about to suggest that she joined him in one when he was suddenly startled by an appalling glassy crash from the kitchen.

'I'd better go,' he said. 'Please excuse me.'

The sight of Georgina paddling about the kitchen floor in a greyish mess of milk, broken glass and droppings brought all his complicated anguish to the surface in a vitriolic fit of temper. Without knowing really what was happening he did something he had never done before; he picked up Georgina bodily, opened the kitchen door and, shouting, threw her into the yard.

'And don't look at me like that, you sulky idiot! You know quite well it's wrong – you'd clean up the mess too if I had my way.'

The words 'sulky idiot' came flying to the disbelieving Phoebe Spencer like a pair of frenzied fireworks exploding in her face. By the time Mr Plomley was back in the room, inconsequentially murmuring something about 'Frightfully sorry – it was Georgina – didn't know she was back – ' she was already on the point of leaving. She didn't want to be involved in any nasty domestic scene.

Nasty, broody, sulky puss, she thought all the way home, and the house like a pigsty. What do men see in some of them? she asked herself and could, if she had only known, have got the answer from Mr Plomley himself, who was at that moment standing by the harmonium with Georgina in his arms, saying, half in tears:

'Forgive me, dear, please. Georgina please, please forgive me. I didn't, didn't know what I was doing. It was just because someone else was here.'

For the next four or five days Georgina seemed to sulk. She pecked daintily at her morning coffee-beans. The one egg she laid did not seem to Mr Plomley as large and brown and handsome as before.

Mr Plomley, self-reproachful, felt that he himself was to blame for these things. He seemed to see in Georgina's jaundiced eye a reflection of his own ill-temper. Desperately he tried to make it up to her.

'Try to eat a little more mash, dear. I put cream in it this morning. Don't you want it? You'll never feel right if you don't eat, will you? Come on, do try.'

Georgina, eyelids and beak drooping, merely stared at him as if she had the pip.

Mr Plomley tried another tactic. It now occurred to him that Georgina's condition might be much less physical than psychological. Mildly he threatened her.

'You don't want me to send for the vet, do you? You know what happened last time. You didn't much care for *that*, did you?'

Georgina, affecting renewed sulkiness by letting her head droop in a crumbled heap on her breast feathers, seemed to make it clear that she didn't think much of vets either.

'There are times when all of us have to help ourselves,' Mr Plomley said in rather stern fashion. 'It's no use giving way. You must pull yourself together.'

In reply Georgina let out a ragged throaty snarl that might have been a hen-like oath or merely a belch of air. But to Mr Plomley it was yet another sign of sickness. The lustre of her comb had greatly faded. It drooped dreadfully down, like a piece of flabby ham.

'I'll see if I can get some aspirin from Mrs Spencer. One of them mashed up in milk can do no harm.'

In his great preoccupation with Georgina's declining moods he had lost all count of time and when he arrived at the shop two or three minutes later it was to find Phoebe Spencer locking the door and pulling down the blind. He hadn't seen or spoken to her since the afternoon Georgina had disgraced herself and he himself had behaved even more badly in return. Now she seemed pleased, even delighted, to see him standing there and with pleasant alacrity she unlocked the door and let up the blind.

'Just closing, but it's perfectly all right. Come in, come in.'

'It was just some aspirins – awfully sorry to put you about –'

'Not the weeniest bit of trouble. How are things?' she said and provided the answer herself after a rapid rove of her eye. 'You look all in. Had a bad day or something?'

Mr Plomley, who increasingly felt as if he were under the worst afflictions of a hangover, confessed that he actually wasn't quite up to the mark. He was awfully worried about Georgina; she wasn't at all herself these days.

While getting the box of aspirins from behind the counter Phoebe Spencer remarked that the weather had been extra warm for the time of year and it affected some women more than others, didn't it? If this dark insinuation was designed to extract from Mr Plomley the particular nature of Georgina's ailment it failed dismally and completely. Mr Plomley, who knew nothing of female ailments, merely stared.

'Why don't you come in a minute and sit yourself down and relax for a bit? I was just going to get myself a drink or something. What about it? Cuppa tea? – glass of ginger wine? With a drop of brandy in it. Favourite drink of mine.'

Without quite knowing why, Mr Plomley all of a sudden felt that a glass of ginger wine with a drop of brandy in it might be both nectar and salvation. Two minutes later he was sitting in Phoebe Spencer's neat back parlour holding in his hands a glass full of such brilliant amber light that it might have been the distillation of all her flaming orange hair.

'Had the doctor?'

'Oh! no, it hasn't come to that. I've been thinking to myself that it may be more psychological.'

'Oh? How do you mean exactly?'

Another dark stroke fell on the canvas of Phoebe Spencer's mind. The sulky puss, she thought again. Psychological, eh?

'It's hard to explain,' Mr Plomley said and then suddenly heard himself make the most incredible, outrageous of statements. Born of all the day's long irritations it leapt out like a striking serpent before he could do a thing to stop it: 'Oh! let's not talk about her.'

The involuntary callousness of this remark immediately struck him utterly speechless. He felt as if it were not himself speaking. It was a stranger inside him, uttering foreign blasphemies.

'Let them get on with it I say sometimes and then they snap out of it. That's what I used to say to Joe.'

This remark had the sudden effect of inducing a curious air of intimacy between them. Phoebe Spencer smiled at him over the ginger wine, imprisoning him in fruity steadfastness with her large sugary eyes.

In order to get out of this trap Mr Plomley found himself making another unexpected remark, not so much outrageous this time as wholly desperate. He was, he told himself for the fiftieth time in less than a week, in it up to his neck.

'I hope you won't mind my asking – but I hope you won't say anything about Georgina to anybody. You know how people talk – how it gets around.'

'Oh! no, no. Wouldn't dream of it.'

'Good, good. I'm awfully grateful. Presumptuous of me to ask, I suppose –'

'Good Heavens, no. Glad to keep a little secret for someone like you.'

'We like to keep ourselves to ourselves. You know what people are.'

'Yes. I saw all the notices on the gate,' Phoebe Spencer said, and then, sipping ginger wine, looked at him slyly. 'But I thought you said we weren't going to talk about her.'

That was so, Mr Plomley began to confess confusedly, but –

'Still, I don't mind what we talk about as long as I've got someone to talk to,' Phoebe Spencer said. 'I get sick of talking to myself.'

'You don't keep a dog or anything, do you?' Mr Plomley said in another flurried exercise of desperation.

'No. I did think of having a parrot at one time. Soon after Joe died. Just for the company.'

Mr Plomley felt himself recoil at the idea of a parrot for company. They were such pompous birds. Somehow they dominated you.

'They're so expensive I didn't get one in the end. Do you keep any pets?'

'None at all. Unless you'd call Georgina a pet.'

For a second or two Mr Plomley stood on the precipitous verge of confession. Then his courage faded. He sucked hard at ginger wine.

'Call her what you like,' Phoebe Spencer said firmly to herself, but not aloud. 'Pet, my foot. I'd pet her, the slut, the sulky puss.'

Against the chill of the evening Phoebe Spencer had switched on an electric radiator. The room was growing warm. The effect of the ginger wine with the drop of brandy in it was to make Mr Plomley lightly soporific. He suppressed a sudden yawn and at the same time heard Phoebe Spencer say:

'Why don't you shut your eyes for five minutes? You look all in. It would do you good.'

'No really, I mustn't do that. I really must be getting back to Georgina soon.'

'Now, now – you weren't going to talk about Georgina.'

'That's right.'

'Then forget her for a moment. Have another glass of wine.'

'Well, I shouldn't, but perhaps just the merest –'

She filled his glass to the brim. The glow of the fire infused into the amber heart of it a concentrated galaxy of ruby stars. Mr Plomley gazed at them until they seemed to revolve, and then dissolve, into space, the glass slightly tilting in his hand as he did so.

When he woke it was dark outside. For more than a minute, as he struggled to focus the still revolving ruby galaxies in his glass, he clung to a dazed conviction that he was at home, having his nightly bout of whisky, with Georgina comfortably nestling on his lap before the fire.

He could have sworn he actually saw crouched there in the glow of it, the dark brown feathers edged with a ring, almost a decorative halo, of a light rosy gold.

A few seconds later he stretched out and touched Phoebe Spencer's thick orange pyramid of hair and out of sheer habit, as he so often did with Georgina, started to stroke it gently with his hand.

On a dull misty November afternoon he went through the last of a series of painful scenes with Georgina, in the potting shed. Eggs had been falling off dreadfully for the past week or two. An increasing lack of lustre in the comb, together with a continued loss of feathers that made him think she was moulting at the wrong time of the year, gave her the appearance of a slightly wanton hag.

'No, I know you don't like it down here. But here's where you're going to live from now on. It's got to be absolutely intolerable lately.'

The brainlessness of hens is nowhere more clearly seen than in the dividing curve of the beak. When viewed from the side it reveals itself to be nothing more than a grotesque and bony sneer.

'And don't sneer at me like that, my girl,' Mr Plomley said, 'just because you're not in the harmonium. Your box is here now and here you can lay.'

Georgina stood on the potting bench, moodily shuffling her feet, and viewed him with a detached and jealous eye. For a moment he was touched by her shabby and lustreless air into a recollection of the girl she had once been. He suddenly felt sorry for her. He was even now ready to forgive everything and said:

'Oh! I won't neglect you. I'll see you're all right. You'll be taken care of.'

A few moments later he went out into the garden, cut a large autumn cabbage and proceeded to hang it up to the potting shed roof with a length of string. She could peck on this, he told her; the exercise would do her good. She could do with more exercise.

Suddenly, as if these were insulting words, she flew at him. With all the envious and rapacious fury of a woman scorned she flew wildly into his face, aiming the grey sneering beak at his ear. A sudden realization that drips of warm blood were dropping down his neck made him lash out protectively with both hands. A brown storm of feathers filled the air.

All at once, by sheer luck, he caught her by both legs and pinned her against the potting bench. She was quivering and croaking in feathery anguish and he was shaking, too. In fury he held her there and started to say:

'I've a good mind to –'

The words he was about to say were 'wring your damn neck' but as he started to frame them he saw her looking back at him with a challenging glare of an old mistress, as if she were about to say:

'Go on, hit me, you great brute. You've got me down now, haven't you? Hit me.'

With a burst of savage relief he let her go. She flew, squawking, into a cloud of seedy cobwebs, banging her wings against an ancient rope of onions that shed a flight of rustling skins. They fell on the air like panting breath.

Finally he locked her in the potting shed and, still shaking, went across to the shop. His ear was running blood. In his distraction he had forgotten it was early closing day again and to his everlasting surprise he found Phoebe Spencer doing her accounts in the living-room behind the shop, sitting at a table in bright vermilion house-coat loosely tied over a pink nylon slip and with the orange pyramid of hair collapsed into an exceptionally brilliant untidiness about her shoulders, as if she had just been washing it.

She seemed almost to flush at his sudden arrival and started hastily to explain that she'd been having a bath and was sorry she was all untidy and then let out an alarming cry:

'Oh! my goodness, whatever's happened? Your ear's

all blood. Have you been having a fight or something?'
'No,' he said. 'No.'

He sat limply at the table. She fetched soap, towel, and a bowl
of warm water and started to wash his ear. The air was full of a
lazy sort of perfume, as of bath salts, to which he could put no
name. The great orange curtain of Phoebe Spencer's hair kept
falling handsomely down across her shoulders. It too was full
of a drifting sweetness that Mr Plomley found difficult to define but soon the astringency of antiseptic cut across it and
presently the bowl of water was lightly pink with blood.

'It's quite a slash,' she said. 'Looks like barbed wire or something. Were you crawling through a hedge?

The old, long need for confession, Mr Plomley thought, could
no longer be resisted. He said in a low, almost tortured voice:

'It was Georgina. We were quarrelling.'

'She must have done it with a knife!' The surly puss, the
quarrelsome bitch, she thought, she might have killed him.
'She must have been –'

'No,' Mr Plomley confessed, 'she bit me.'

That was even worse! – the cheap, vulgar puss. She wasn't
civilized. Was he going to stand for that sort of thing?

'No,' Mr Plomley said. 'I'm not. Not any longer. It's
finished. It's all over.'

'But whatever made her do a terrible thing like that? That's
a savage gash across your ear.'

In a low, humiliated voice Mr Plomley allowed himself
another confession.

'She's jealous of you. It's been coming to the boil for weeks
now.'

'Jealous of me? But she's never even met me! She's never
even seen me!'

'She's jealous all the same.'

'But did you ever talk to her about me?'

'No. I never said a word.'

'Then how in Heaven's name can she be jealous of me? –
someone she's never even seen?'